★　　★　　★　　★　　★　　★　　★

I tried to ignore the shadow over me, but you can't do that when it belongs to the heavyweight champion of the world.

"He dead?" Joe Louis said, breathing heavily. Louis was wearing blue shorts and an extra-large white T-shirt stained with sweat. His feet were bare. I wondered how I was going to tell Anne about the massive brown figure casting his shadow over me and the badly beaten body.

It was the last day of May 1942, a Sunday. I knew Joe Louis was a corporal in the U.S. Army. I also knew John Barrymore had died on Friday and that the Cubs had just purchased Jimmie Foxx from the Red Sox. I knew the RAF had just blitzed Cologne and that I had $15 in my pocket and nothing in the bank.

"You know who I am?" Louis asked.

"Max Baer," I said.

The Toby Peters Mysteries

DOWN FOR THE COUNT

A TOBY PETERS MYSTERY

STUART M. KAMINSKY

THE MYSTERIOUS PRESS

New York • London
Tokyo • Sweden • Milan

MYSTERIOUS PRESS EDITION

This Mysterious Press Edition is published by arrangement with
the author.

Cover design and illustration by Tom McKeveney

Mysterious Press books are published in association with
Warner Books, Inc.
666 Fifth Avenue
New York, N.Y. 10103
A Warner Communications Company

Printed in the United States of America

First Mysterious Press Printing: June, 1990

10 9 8 7 6 5 4 3 2 1

*For Don Siegel, who started it
all for me*

The Clock Strikes one that just struck two
Some schism in the Sum—
A Vagabond from Genesis
Has wrecked the Pendulum—

—Emily Dickinson

1

I tried to ignore the shadow over me, but you can't do that when it belongs to the heavyweight champion of the world.

"He dead?" Joe Louis said, breathing heavily. Louis was wearing blue shorts and an extra-extra large white T-shirt stained with sweat. His feet were bare.

"Down for the count," I said.

About a quarter-mile down the shore some girls were giggling in the surf, the late sun hitting their tanned bodies, their voices bubbling through the white waves hitting the beach and the corpse I was kneeling next to. I looked away from the girls and out over the ocean at the sun heading for Japan. I wondered how I was going to tell Anne about the massive brown figure in the wet sand casting his shadow over me and the badly beaten body. There wasn't much face left on the body, but there wasn't any doubt about who it was.

Ralph Howard had always dressed tastefully, conservatively. Even now with sand, salt water, and pinkish blood staining the tan panama suit, the corpse had Ralph's touch.

I looked up at Louis, who waited for me to say something. This is as far as you can go, I thought. The edge of the U.S.A. When you get this far you either jump in or turn around and ask yourself where you've been. It was at this philosophical point that I could no longer ignore Louis's hands. His knuckles were white and tight and dabbed with blood.

"Hey wait," he said, pointing a finger at me. "You ain't . . . I didn't hit this man."

The falling sun caught drops of sweat or sea in his black hair and made him look as if he had been through about five or six tough rounds. There was a kind of softness to his brown, round face, and his full lips gave him a perpetual pout. I wondered what I would do if he simply decided to turn around and run down the beach. I'm five-nine, and at a little under 160 and carrying forty-eight years there was no way I was going to keep that man from running away. Granted I have a face that looks as if it's been hit by a fist or two, a nose that vaguely remembers cartilage, and eyes that stay with you. I saw that face every morning when I remembered to shave, but Louis had seen tougher ones.

I got up, brushed sand from my new suit, and glanced down at the corpse, its well-brushed white hair flecked with blood.

"What happened here?" I said, looking at Louis across the body. I did it with a sigh, trying to sound official. I'd been a cop once. My brother was a cop still. I knew the routine. If Louis thought I was the law, I might keep him there.

He looked down at the body and then back over his shoulder in the general direction of the giggling girls. I glanced at them. Maybe he was waiting for the pair to come running over, kicking up ocean spray and giving him an alibi, but they were far away and not even looking in our direction.

"I was running," he said. His face came back to mine.

"From what?" I said.

He shifted his weight, and his pectorals showed against his wet T-shirt. If I'd had my gun, I might have been able to stop him, but the gun was back in the Ford up near the house on the hill.

"From nothing," he said. Actually, he said, "Fum nuthin'," but I had no trouble understanding him. I considered reaching in my pocket for a notebook, but my pocket notebook was a little job with spirals, and I knew the spiral had unraveled. I didn't want to find myself chasing little lined sheets of paper in the Pacific Ocean. So, I waited for Louis to say something else. We might have waited through the entire Second World War if I hadn't given him a little prompting.

"You didn't kill him. You were just out doing roadwork on the beach in Santa Monica, and you came across a corpse. Coincidentally, you just happened to come across it after you had bloodied your knuckles on a helpless antelope that accidentally crossed your path."

Louis looked down at his knuckles. He was still panting, but not as heavily. It was more a series of deep sighs.

"There were two guys," he said now, looking up toward the road away from the beach. We both looked, but there weren't two guys. There wasn't anybody.

"Two guys," I repeated while he pulled his thoughts together.

"Big guys," he went on slowly. "They were standing right here near . . ." He nodded toward the corpse. "He kin of yours or something?"

"Looks as if my wife's husband got himself killed," I explained, but it didn't make sense to Louis, who had a lot to deal with at the moment.

"Two men, big men. They were standing over the body," I reminded him. Surf splashed a sudden wave, and I had to jump toward dry sand to keep my new shoes from getting wetter. Louis just stood there and let the waves hit him ankle high. The corpse took a turn for the surf.

Rather than take a chance on losing Ralph, I grabbed the body and tried to lug it away from the shore. I grunted with the waterlogged weight and pulled him an inch or two before Louis reached down with one hand, grabbed the corpse's well-pressed jacket, and pulled him about five feet onto the dry sand next to a white wooden post plunked down in the sand. A triangular sign on the post read: BE VIGILANT. NO

LANDINGS ARE AUTHORIZED ON THIS BEACH. IMME-
DIATELY REPORT ANY BOAT ACTUALLY LANDING PERSONS
ON SHORE HERE TO THE NEAREST MILITARY OR NAVAL
POST AND TO THE SHERIFF AND POLICE FORCES. U.S. COAST
GUARD. At the bottom of the sign was the emblem of the
Auto Club of Southern California.

I was panting now. I wondered how many of those people I was supposed to report Ralph's body to.

"You ain't the police," Louis said.

"No," I agreed. "I'm a private detective. Name's Peters,
Toby Peters. I think I got hired by my ex-wife a few hours ago
to keep her second husband from winding up with his face
smashed and taking a fully clothed dip in the ocean."

"Sorry," Louis said sincerely, putting his bloody hands
up.

"Hey, I didn't love him," I said. "But in a minute or two
we're going to have to go up to that nice house and explain
that Ralph is dead and tell his widow something about what
happened."

"I don't know for sure. Two men standing over the guy is
all. I came running to see if I could help and they went for
me. They knew what they was doing. They done some fighting."

"And?" I pushed, looking toward the house, wondering
when Anne or the servant or somebody might look out the
window and wonder what the hell was happening.

"I hurt them," he said simply.

"And that's what happened to your hands?"

He nodded slowly, his eyes on mine, not blinking, sizing
me up. I did not want him to hurt me.

"Okay," I sighed. "We go up to the house, have a bad
hour or two. You describe the guys to the cops and you go
running back into the sunset, only by then it will be moonlight."

"Can't do it," he said, chewing on his lower lip. "I'm not
supposed to be here."

It was the last day of May 1942, a Sunday. I knew Louis was a corporal in the U.S. Army. I also knew John Barrymore had died on Friday and that the Cubs had just purchased Jimmie Foxx from the Red Sox. I knew the RAF had just blitzed Cologne and that I had $15 in my pocket and nothing in the bank, but I didn't know where Joe Louis was supposed to be.

"You know who I am?" he asked.

"Max Baer," I said. He was about to correct me when I held up a hand to stop him. "You're the champ," I said.

"Tha's right." He nodded. The sun was taking a fast dive. I looked up at the three-story house where Anne lived and saw a light go on. Somebody, maybe Anne, would wander over to the window and . . .

"I got to trust you," he said, rubbing his forehead. The girls weren't giggling anymore. They were gone and a cool evening wind came in from the water, smelling like fish and far away. "I was with a friend who lives down that way."

He pointed down that way along the beach. The shadows of a dozen nicely spaced houses were behind him.

"So, we tell your friend. Your friend tells the cops you were just visiting. You have a reason for being here. You've got no reason to turn Ralph into ground beef and—"

"My friend's a lady," he said. "A white lady."

I didn't say anything.

"A white lady lots of people know."

He had been ahead of me for a quarter of a beat, but I caught up fast. Louis was the clean-cut Negro American, the super patriot who had enlisted as a private when the war began, the family man, a credit to his race, as one sports writer put it, but another one amended that, saying, "Yes, the human race."

"Yeah," I said brilliantly.

"I'm still married to my wife, Marva," he said softly. I could hardly see his face now. He stood with his arms folded, his muscles rippled. "And . . ."

"And you're no saint," I finished.

"No saint at all," he agreed. "Damn, no sense in talking. I got to do what's right. You got a mama?"

"Not since I was eight," I said, wondering what the hell we were getting into.

"Well mine's telling me to go up to that house with you and take what's coming," Louis said. "Le's go before I change my mind."

He took a quick step past me and the posted sign we had propped the body against and accidentally kicked sand into the battered face of the corpse. As he passed me, Louis smelled like the YMCA on Hope Street in L.A. where I worked out. He smelled like the hundreds of fights I'd gone to at the Olympic, and he smelled like a human being who was sweating fear but facing it.

"Hold it," I said. He turned a dozen yards from me. "How'd you like to hire a private detective?"

"Huh?" was his answer.

"You hire me," I explained, "and I work for you. I do my best to see to it that your name stays out of this, if I can."

An angry look crossed his face. Something that never showed in the pre-fight and after-the-fight photos. In those Louis always looked calm, distant, like he was thinking of a song he had forgotten.

"Wait a minute," I went on, holding my hands up to keep him from me as he strode back down to where I stood. "I'm not blackmailing you, just trying to give myself some kind of professional cover." He was about a straight left jab away from me when I finished my argument. "Let's call it five bucks."

Louis stopped, tilted his head to one side to examine me as if I were a picture hung wrong.

"You crazy, man?" he said.

"Probably," I agreed. "Let's just say I'm a fan, a patriot, and I believe you. We got a deal or we got a deal?"

"I don't know," he said, looking at the dead body, but it wasn't about to give him advice.

Over his shoulder I could see a door opening in Anne's house, the splay of light hitting a figure who had stepped out.

"Well make up your mind fast," I said. "Someone is coming. My name is Peters, Toby Peters. I'm in the phone book. Private Investigators. My office is downtown, Hoover and Ninth. You call me tomorrow."

"You *must* be a crazy man," he said again, but this time there was a little smile in the corner of his mouth. He took off down the beach and I watched him. He ran along the shore in the wet sand, the waves hitting his toes. He was fast and sure. He ran a hell of a lot better than he talked.

The figure from the house was moving down toward me, not too fast but steady, curious. It wasn't a woman. I kneeled again at the body and quickly went through the pockets. A wallet, Ralph's name on the driver's license, a picture of him and Anne grinning. In the picture, his teeth were white and even. There was a stack of bills in the wallet, twenties, tens, fives, easily more than a few hundred dollars. In another pocket was a notebook, a small, leather-covered notebook. A little water had gotten to it, and some of the pages stuck together.

"Why don't we just hold it right there?" the voice behind me called. He was about a pool-cue length away from me, holding a gun level at my stomach. There wasn't much hair on his head, a few wisps. The night breeze caught them and made them dance crazily, but there was nothing crazy in his eyes. He wasn't young, maybe fifty-five, but he had been around. Even the neat, well-pressed blue suit couldn't let him pass for executive material. The face was dark, hard like a tree. It wasn't his face or the gun that clinched things. No, it was the way he looked down at the shredded corpse, let out a little "tsk" of regret and turned his attention to me.

"You know what you cost me, cheap shot?" he said shaking his head.

"I've got a feeling I'm going to find out."

He came another step toward me still shaking his head, his few hairs still flying wildly.

"You took a meal ticket right out of my pocket," he said, patting his pocket as if I had literally taken a piece of cardboard from him. "You know what I was picking up per week for keeping him in one piece?"

He was about four feet from me now. He was either going to take a chance on getting close enough to hit me and give himself some satisfaction, or he was going to play it smart and stay far enough away so I couldn't do anything dumb like go for his gun. He decided to be smart and stopped.

"How much were you picking up?" I asked, not sure myself if I wanted him to keep coming or back off.

"One hundred a week," he said.

"Dollars?" I asked.

"What the hell else?" he said angrily.

"Dog biscuits," I tried.

"You're a goddamn comic, aren't you?" he said, holding the gun out. "You turn a guy into chopped liver and you make jokes? I'm no youngster here, you know?"

"I can see that," I said.

"No youngster," he repeated, shaking his head sadly. "You think a lot of good things come along like this?"

"No," I said, this time speaking from experience.

"No is right. Now what the hell do I do for chrissake? Do I shoot you? I never shot anybody. I'm just a guy doing a job. I'm supposed to keep him alive and now look at him. He's not alive."

I looked at the body, but I knew full well he was dead.

"Why don't we just go up to the house and call the cops?" I suggested. "First we tell Mrs. Howard and then we call the cops."

Most of the remaining light now was from the open door

of the house. The shadows of the man and me and the corpse were long. The ocean cleared its throat behind us.

"Who was that running away?" he said. "And how do you know Mrs. Howard?"

"I didn't see anybody running, and I used to be married to her. My name's Toby Peters. What's yours?"

"Carl Paitch, but my giving you my name doesn't make us buddies. I still figure you for doing Howard over there."

"So?" I prodded.

"So," he said with a shrug and finally patted down his flying hair. "Who really gives a shit. You know what I mean? Let's go up to the house."

He started to lead the way, thought better of it, and waved me forward with his gun. His hair was dancing again by the time I passed him and started up the sandy hillside. It had been easier going down than it was climbing up. My shoes were full of sand when I got to the open door and stepped in. I reached down to take off my shoes and Paitch almost bumped into me. I could have taken the gun from him then, but what would have been the point?

"Things like this happen to me all the goddamn time," he said, plopping into a chair in the little hallway. It was one of those old-looking chairs with fuzzy dark red on the seat and old dark wood all over. His gun was now pointing at the small Persian carpet.

"I'd say it was Ralph Howard it happened to this time," I said, dumping sand out the door onto the small wooden porch.

"That's not what I meant," he explained, not looking at me. "I just can't hold onto a job. The big ones always get away. You know what I'm saying?"

"The big ones always get away," I said, putting my shoes back on.

"That's what I'm saying," he repeated.

"How about calling the cops and getting Mrs. Howard?" I said.

Paitch's wild few strands of hair were draped over his eyes. Ralph Howard had picked one hell of a soft banana to keep him alive.

"The police?" came a voice from above. I looked up at Anne coming down the stairway. I hadn't seen her for a few months. She had dropped a few pounds. Her black hair was swept back and she was wearing white, all white like Lana Turner in *The Postman Always Rings Twice*. She looked better than she ever had when she'd been married to me, but there were good reasons. She might not be looking quite so good in a few seconds.

"Anne," I said, taking a step toward her. She saw something in my eyes and stopped three steps above me so she could keep from contact, keep from knowing.

"What happened . . . Ralph?"

Her eyes were brown and wet as always, and I knew if I wandered through the house it would be brown and white and clean, everything in place, a world made neat as Anne always wanted, a world far different from the one she had shared with me. I was enough chaos for one lifetime. Ralph had been money and order and reliability, and here I was again to leave coffee grounds on the rug.

"Dead," called Paitch, trying to rally his minimal resources. "Out on the beach. Someone beat the crap out of him, Mrs. Howard. I didn't even know he—"

"How about calling the cops, Carl," I said without looking at him.

Anne's face was calm and still and white. She let her tongue touch her lower lip, one of the few signs of emotion she was willing to show or couldn't control.

"Toby, I . . ."

"This guy was standing over him, Mrs. Howard," Paitch said, waving his gun in my general direction. "And another guy was running away."

"Make the call, Carl," I repeated.

"You know there was nothing I could do about it," he

rambled on. "I got to take time to eat too, don't I? A man's got to eat, doesn't he?"

"No he doesn't, Carl," I said. "The telephone."

"Call the police, Mr. Paitch," Anne said firmly, her eyes still on me.

"I'm calling the cops," Paitch said decisively as if he had just thought of it. "Right now." And he turned and went through the door of a darkened room behind him. Anne and I didn't say anything for a second or two, just listened to Paitch bungle into odd pieces of furniture, find the light, and finally pick up the phone.

"I'm not going to break, Toby," she said softly, putting her head forward. She had clasped her hands tightly together, and the effort to keep it in sent a shiver through her.

"I know, Anne," I said.

Paitch's voice wasn't booming but it was loud and clear from inside the room.

"Ralph Howard. Right. Yes. I'm sure. You don't have a face like that if you're alive I'm telling you."

Anne's eyes blinked, and I hurried over to close the door where Paitch was making the call. We could still hear his voice, but not the words. Anne had taken the last two steps down and I moved to her, held out my hand, but she unclasped hers and held up a palm to keep me away. I knew what she was saying. A touch from me, maybe from anyone, would break her and she didn't want to break, at least not yet, maybe not at all.

"Let's go in here," she said, turning to a room off the hallway. I followed her and stood in the doorway as she turned on the lights. The room was brown and white, and clean. No children or oafs treaded here, just civilized people, but it wasn't a civilized person who had done the job on the corpse on the beach.

"Would you like something to drink?" she said, looking around, unable to remember for the moment where the drinks were. If she weren't about to crack, she would remember that the beer I drink isn't found in a liquor cabinet. "A Pepsi?" she asked, striding toward a cabinet, brown and very old, in a corner. The floor was finely polished dark wood with a white and brown checkered rug, a big plush checkerboard in the center.

"No, thanks," I said.

"Right," she went on, still walking. "I'll have something."

"You want me to get it for you?"

"No," she said. "I want something to do."

"How about crying?" I asked softly.

"Maybe later," she said. "Definitely later. But we've got business now before the police come."

I shut up, was careful not to step on the rug, and stood patiently while she slowly made herself a drink, took a sip, shuddered, and turned back toward me across the long room. The light from two lamps was dim, and her face was hidden in darkness, but her voice had a sob in it and I was sure her eyes were more than usually moist.

"I'm not much of a drinker," she said, tossing her dark hair back and looking into the amber liquid in her glass as if it held some secret.

"I know," I answered. "Anne . . ."

"I know," she said with a sigh, looking up at me. "About a week ago someone tried to kill Ralph. I saw it, Toby, I was there. We were crossing Melrose on a Saturday. We had just come out of Marko's after dinner. A car came right at us, no other traffic, nothing. Right at us. Ralph pushed me back and the car missed him by inches. Ralph was shaken, but he said something about a drunk driver. I saw the driver's face. He wasn't drunk."

"What did he look like?" I asked.

Anne swirled her drink and continued to avoid my eyes. "A man. I don't know. He looked tough, dark. I don't remember, Toby, and before you ask, I don't think I would recognize him again. The next day, Ralph hired Paitch."

Ralph could have done a hell of a lot better than Paitch, I thought, but there was no point in saying it now.

"And everything was fine till today, which is why you called me?" I said, wanting to sit on the harder arm of one of the chairs. The cushion I was on was too soft, and my bad back gave me a very small warning. I shifted my weight.

"No," she said, dragging out the word. "There were signs all the time since that car tried to hit him. He was nervous, his mind, memory couldn't stay in the room. And he began to have some problems at work."

Ralph worked for Trans World Airlines, a vice president or something like it. He had been with the company since it started and was greatly respected by Howard Hughes, though I had only Anne's word for that. She too had worked for TWA, where she had met Ralph. I had met husband number two a few times.

"What kind of problems?" I prompted, realizing that Anne had paused, her own thoughts wandering. But she came back strong.

"Nothing terrible," she said. "Just a drop in his attention. A contract he was handling for replacement parts was delayed and resulted in a cost rise. Costs are rocketing since the war. He spent more and more time on his new hobby."

"Which was?" I asked, forcing myself not to look at my watch, which wasn't very difficult. The watch had belonged to my father. It was accidentally right about twice during a normal day. I wanted to prompt her again, get something more before the police arrived or Paitch decided to walk in, but I played the role of patient listener.

"Boxing," she sighed, looking up at me defiantly, expecting some wise-ass comment.

"Ralph was boxing?" I said.

"Ralph had bought contracts or parts of contracts of some professional boxers. I think he had quite a bit of money invested."

I couldn't sit a second longer or my back would have

locked. I pushed myself up and kept my voice low, stepping toward her.

"That doesn't sound like Ralph," I said. "Not that I knew Ralph very well mind you, but it doesn't—"

"It wasn't" she agreed, finishing off her drink in two quick gulps. Then she laughed, a small laugh. "I haven't drunk in years, Toby. Do you know why? Because drinking makes you fat."

I thought about all the skinny drunks my landlord was always hauling out of the dark corners of the Farraday Building on Hoover, where I had my office. Maybe alcohol made women fat and men skinny? I didn't share the insight with Anne.

"I don't have to worry about that any more though, do I?"

I didn't answer and she went on.

"I own this house," she said, looking at the ceiling where a cone of light from the lamp made a path to the far corner. "Ralph had a big insurance policy and a bank account. I don't have to worry about how I look any more."

"Annie," I said, wanting to reach out and touch her. "You're not going to change. I couldn't change you. You couldn't change me."

"We will see, Tobias," she said, biting her lower lip. "We will see."

The idea of Ralph getting mixed up with boxing reminded me of Joe Louis. Had Louis been there to see Ralph? Maybe it wasn't just an unlucky break for the Brown Bomber. Maybe I had put my foot through a rotten egg.

"Do you know why he got interested in boxing?" she said, sounding slightly drunk. There was no way the alcohol could have worked that quickly. She wanted it to happen, needed it, and had helped it along.

I shook my head.

"Because of you. He never said so, but it didn't take much to figure it out. You're tough, had more fights than I want to think about, and he knew you were interested in box-ing."

Interested was a mild word and Anne knew it.

"Ralph was a gentle, determined businessman," she went on, looking at me angrily as if I was about to mount an argu-ment. "He was . . ."

"Everything I'm not," I finished.

"Just about," she said. "I wanted him because of that. I loved him because of that and the poor . . ." She sobbed, shaking her head. "The poor . . ."

"Bastard," I supplied.

". . . thought he had to compete with you."

"Hey, Annie," I said, now no more than a foot from her. "I'm not responsible for Ralph getting killed. I've come close to being responsible for me getting killed, but Ralph packed his own suitcase."

"He expected to get killed tonight," she said. Her fin-gers had gone white around the fragile, now empty glass. I reached out and took it from her. My fingers touched her but she didn't pull back. I put the glass on a table and waited.

"He got a call this afternoon," she said. "I don't know who or what or why. I heard the phone ring. I know he an-swered, and then he came to me. I was upstairs reading. He said he had to go out. He looked, I don't know, strange, ner-vous. He told me he loved me and I made some joke about knowing it, but now I think he was saying good-bye or at least a just-in-case good-bye. He kissed me and went out, didn't say where he was going or who he was going to meet. I got frightened, Toby, and I called you. But I called too late."

I touched her arm. She shuddered and then leaned against me. She smelled like old memories and tears, and her breasts were warm through her white dress, and I felt guilty but what the hell, I hugged her.

My timing was great. While I held her a voice came from behind me.

"I don't want to disturb anything here, but are you the folks with the body?"

Anne pulled away, and I turned to face a beefy man with a red face. He was somewhere in his fifties and looked like a bloated salami. He hadn't taken his hat off. His rumpled suit was dark, and the hat almost matched. It sat on the back of his head, his gray hair matted in front of it and over his forehead.

"This is the widow," I said to the cop, who I recognized but didn't know by name. My brother is a captain at the Wilshire, and years back I'd been a uniform in Glendale. Even without the connection, I'd met most of the cops who had been around for a while. This guy worked out of Santa Monica. He had an Irish name and the reputation for not being fond of work.

"I know you," he said, pointing a finger at me and stepping in. I could feel his presence doing something to Anne, and I knew what it was. The cop was behaving the way I usually did, and I knew how she reacted to that.

"I assume you are a policeman," she said firmly.

The cop stopped and looked at her with the trace of a sneer.

"And you're the . . ." he said.

"I'm the widow," she finished. "And you are an insensitive heap of offal. How did you get in here?"

"Door was open," the cop said. "I just walked in and found you and . . . I know who you are, Peters, the private keyhole who got into all kinds of shit in Venice a few years ago."

"And I know who you are," I said, remembering. "You're a pickled cop named Meara. Your name just came to me when you got close enough for me to smell the cheap whiskey."

Meara smiled and shook his head. "I heard you had a big mouth," he said. "I guess you use it to console widows too."

"Meara," I said with a grin, "how would you like a nose like mine?"

"I'll ask you a different one," he countered. "How'd you like an hour with me back at the station? Just a quiet cup of tea and some literary talk in our library."

"Officer," Anne said softly.

"Sergeant," Meara corrected.

"Sergeant," she said, stepping past me to face him. "Mr. Peters is an old friend. In fact, Mr. Peters and I were once married. I called him earlier today to come out here and see if he could help Ralph, my husband, to stay alive. Now don't you think your time would be better spent looking at the . . . at my husband?"

I started to put my arm around her, but she sensed it and stepped away.

"Got a man doing just that," Meara said. "Fella who seems to work here met us outside and led my man down to the corpse. I thought I'd just check out the bereaved and get some background."

He gave me a less than cheerful look and plopped down in an armchair.

"Sorry if I jumped to anything," he said with no touch of regret in his voice. If anything, his sarcasm had increased. "Just doing my job. It's been a tough day."

"We sympathize with you, Meara," I said.

Voices were coming from the hallway, and Paitch appeared with a young man dressed exactly like Meara. There was something wacky about him, but I couldn't tell what it was right away, not until he stepped over to Meara's side with Paitch behind him. One of his eyes was looking into a dark corner. The other was looking at me. I figured that the one on me was the real one. It was the other that had kept him 4F. At least that's what I figured until he started to talk, and then I subtracted 4F from his IQ and got about a 9D, my shoe size.

"He's dead, Sergeant," the young man said.

"Thank you, Officer Belleforte," Meara said, his eyes

moving from me to Anne. "We did have some evidence that he might be."

"Face is smashed to hell," Belleforte said.

Anne started to sag at my side.

"You want me to call the Medical Examiner?" Belleforte said, looking at Meara and the coffee table ten feet away.

"Either that or leave the body out there as a tourist attraction or to scare away the Japs if they decide to land," Meara said, enjoying himself. He had his hands folded on his belly.

"I'll call the examiner," Belleforte decided, moving toward the door. "There's sand all over him. You want me to get samples?"

"If a man is found dead on the beach," Meara sighed, "there is a good chance that some sand will be found on his body."

"But," countered Belleforte, "what if he was killed someplace else and brought here? The sand might be different."

Meara closed his eyes, unclasped his hands, and made a shooing gesture toward the door. Belleforte hurried out of the room.

"Boy's head is filled with sand," he said. "That's what we've got to work with because of the Japs and the Nazis."

Paitch had placed himself behind and to one side of Meara, probably hoping to be out of sight and awareness.

"And you," Meara said, opening his eyes and pointing over his shoulder without looking. "What the hell do you do around here?"

"Me?" asked Paitch, looking at me and Anne to be sure the question was his to field.

"No," said Meara. "One of the other six fellas with you."

Paitch rubbed his nose and touched his face and let the little finger of his left hand touch his lower lip. "I'm Mr. Howard's bodyguard," he said almost in a whisper. "I mean I was his bodyguard. I don't think anybody's going to pay me to guard his body now that it's dead."

"Okay," I said. "That's enough, Meara. Mrs. Howard isn't up to this act. You want to play Old King Cole, do it without her."

But he wasn't going to do it without her, and it turned into a long, long night.

2

It was after two in the morning when I got to Mrs. Plaut's Boarding House on Heliotrope in Hollywood, where I rented a small, less than luxury room. Since I didn't want a luxury room, I didn't mind putting up with Mrs. Plaut, about whom more anon. I got that "anon" from my next-door neighbor Gunther, who happens to be a midget. Gunther is my friend, has been since I helped get him off a murder charge back in 1940. Gunther had gotten me into Mrs. Plaut's at a time when rooms were hard to come by. Now they were impossible to find.

The house was dark when I walked up the gray wooden front steps. I had found a parking space across the street, a little close to a driveway, but what the hell. Somewhere far away a dog was whimpering.

I let myself in, took off my shoes, and tiptoed across the creaking floor toward the stairs. Mrs. Plaut was several thousand years old, had been for generations. She was almost deaf though she had the senses of a movie Indian. She felt every vibration in the house. Getting past her, day or night, was a challenge I had seldom met. The eighty-watt bulb encased in a snowy white cover overhead snapped on, and she stood in the doorway of her rooms, a tiny, frail figure in an oversized maroon robe. Her hands were folded against her chest.

"Mr. Peelers," she said loudly. "Do you know what time it is?"

"No," I said, looking at my watch, which suggested seven

of some day, year, or century that had already passed or might never come.

"It is nearly three in the A.M.," she supplied. "And you are not being considerate of the feelings of others. You are waking people."

Her little chin pointed at me and I knew I would never suggest to her that the only one waking anyone up was her. Behind her in the darkness of her rooms I could hear her recently acquired canary, Sweet Alice, chirping away.

"Mr. Hill must get up at six to deliver the mail," she said. "And I will be preparing breakfast at that same hour. What do you have to say to that?"

There was nothing to say to it. I wanted to get to my room, take off some of my clothes, and plop on the mattress I had placed on the floor to keep my back from living rigor mortis. I shrugged and tried to look sheepishly contrite, which probably made me look instead something like a bulldog imitating Baby Sandy.

"Have you been killing persons again?" she asked.

There seemed to be some question in Mrs. Plaut's mind about just what I did for a living. At times she seemed to think I was an exterminator, not an unreasonable conclusion based on bits and pieces she might have picked up in the two years I had lived in this bit of heaven on Heliotrope, but she had also latched onto the idea that I did some editing for a publisher she never quite identified. For more than a year I had been reading and editing her massive family history. It was easier than trying to explain things to her.

"I've killed no one today, Mrs. Plaut," I said. "Cross my heart and hope to die."

"Don't do that," she said, shaking her wrinkled hand at me. "Cousin Christopher did that. Crossed his heart and hoped to die and fell down dead. He had just sworn to his wife, Cousin Roweana, that he had never lusted after the Mexican woman who did the cleaning. Do not cross your heart like that, Mr. Peelers."

I took a few shuffling steps toward the stairs, but Mrs. Plaut, robe flowing, outflanked me. I shrugged, a tired, beaten man, and waited for whatever was coming.

"Gas will soon be rationed," she said.

"That a fact?" I said.

"I have told you about your occasional lack of respect," she said.

"I apologize," I said, trying to ease past her, but she was having none of it.

"I think it reasonable that you contribute some stamps to the upkeep of this house," she said.

A week earlier she had wheedled my sugar stamps out of me, but gas was going too far.

"You don't even drive," I said. "You haven't had your Ford out of the garage since 1920-something."

"Twenty-eight," she said. "Husband died in twenty-seven, but the vehicle is ready as am I."

"We'll discuss it in the A.M.," I said.

"And," she went on after I had earned a minor victory by finally getting past her and up four stairs, "I would like to know how you have reacted to the revisions on the chapter about the Davis mining ventures. My uncle is still lost in that mine outside of Turlock."

There was no chance that her uncle was still lost in the mine, since the incident had taken place forty years earlier and Uncle Case was already sixty when he wandered into the darkness in search of silver.

"Sanctuary," I said, putting my palms up and showing my shoes in one hand.

"You are on the verge of being a hopeless case, Mr. Peelers," she said, turning her back on me. Sweet Alice chirped on happily. As Mrs. Plaut turned away from me I could see the words *Horn of Plenty* in white letters on the back of her red robe. I hoped I would never be curious enough to try to ask what those words might mean. There are some mysteries better left unsolved.

I got to the top landing, moved past the pay phone, and groped my way along the wall. Mrs. Plaut had turned off the downstairs light and there was none upstairs.

"Toby?" came Gunther's voice out of the darkness, his Swiss accent clear even in the single word.

There was some moonlight coming through the window at the end of the hallway, but my eyes hadn't adjusted to it yet. I stopped, not wanting to trip over Gunther or knee him in the nose.

"You are all right?" he said.

"I'm okay, Gunther," I said.

"I heard Mrs. Plaut," he said, "and I couldn't help noticing the time. I hope you don't think I'm being overly concerned."

"No," I said, figuring that his voice was coming from the doorway of his room, next to mine. "It's been a long night. Ralph Howard seems to have gotten himself murdered."

Gunther had come with me to Anne and Ralph's wedding. I hadn't been able to face it alone. At first Anne had thought I had brought the dapper little man as a joke, an insult, but Gunther's politeness had overcome that and he had gotten along well with Ralph and Anne though the visit had been brief.

"That is very terrible," he said. "Mrs. Howard must be most overly distraught."

"Most overly," I agreed.

"And who did this?" he asked. I could now make him out in the moonlight. He was perfectly shaped and, as I knew he would be, wearing a robe underneath which would be well-pressed pajamas. The last pair of pajamas I owned had been torn in my mother's wringer washer when I was six or seven. She had died a little after that. I've slept in underwear since then.

"Cops don't know yet," I said. "I'm going to do some checking. I think I better get some sleep now, Gunther. Let's talk about it in the morning. How about a late breakfast, let's say ten in my room?"

"I shall bring the coffee," he said. "Good night, Toby . . . and I'm most sorry about how your former wife must be feeling."

"Thanks, Gunther," I said, finding the door to my room.

I went in, closed the door behind me, and in the darkness imagined Joe Louis throwing a short right-left-right combination to Ralph's face and following it with solid punches, probably when Ralph was lying on his back unconscious. It wasn't right. I wasn't sure the police would see that it didn't make sense, especially Meara, who was ready to nail Ralph's murder on anyone who had a wooden chest and no good alibi. When I had left, Meara had begun seriously working on Paitch as a suspect. He hadn't given up on Anne and me being in some kind of conspiracy, but it was Paitch's turn. I had told Anne I wanted to stay, but she insisted that I go. I didn't like leaving her with Meara. He was the kind of methodical plodder who would simply go through everyone in Ralph's life one person at a time, suspecting them all. Meara was a thorough son of a bitch.

I didn't turn on the light. There was no reason to. I knew where the sofa was with the two doilies. I knew where the alcove was with my wooden table and two chairs, where the small refrigerator stood, where the Beech-Nut Gum clock looked down from the wall, humming through the night, and where my mattress lay waiting. I didn't grope for the closet, just took off my jacket and shirt, massaged my chest through my undershirt, and took off my pants, checking to be sure that the notebook I had taken from Ralph's pocket and the photograph of Ralph that Anne had given me were still there. They were. I tossed my pants, jacket, and shirt in the general direction of the sofa, sat on the mattress and took off my socks. My mouth and teeth felt fuzzy and the black stubble on my chin was hard and bristly with more gray hairs than I wanted to see. I should have found my toothbrush and Dr.

Lyon's powder and made my way down the hall to the community bathroom, but I didn't. I'd scrub myself in the morning. Right now I wanted to sleep. I found the blanket crumpled at the top of the mattress, spread it out, located the first pillow for the back of my head and the extra pillow to hold onto to keep from rolling over on my stomach and destroying my back. I tried not to imagine that the pillow was Anne as I fell asleep.

A gentle knock on the door woke me up, and I rolled over on my back to look up at the Beech-Nut Gum clock on the wall. It was ten on the nose.

"Come in, Gunther," I said over a sandy tongue, and in he came balancing a tray on his right hand and opening the door with his left.

"I have awakened you," he said.

"It's time for awakening," I said, sitting up and rubbing my scratchy chin. "I've got a client."

"That is good," Gunther said, closing the door and carrying the tray to my table. Gunther was dressed, as always, as if he were the president of UCLA. He wore a three-piece tan suit with a white shirt and tie. The tie was light brown with vertical tan stripes. His key chain, tastefully silver, dangled from his watch pocket. He reminded me of Alice's white rabbit.

"What's all that?" I said, getting to a sitting position.

"Breakfast," he answered. "Toast lightly buttered with orange marmalade, coffee, and a newspaper."

I got up, allowing the smell of coffee to get through to me.

"The coffee will remain hot," Gunther said. "Why do you not freshen up for the morning while I find you a clean cereal bowl?"

I could take the hint. If my odor matched the way I knew I looked, only a Main Street bum would be willing to look at me across the table. I staggered out of the room and down the hall, trying to get used to the sunlight. That was easier than what I faced in the mirror. There were a few more gray wiry strands in my wild hair and stubble. My thrice-broken nose looked even more like a carelessly discarded piece of bubble gum than it had the last time I had looked. Lava soap, a shave with what was left of my Molle shaving cream and Gillette blade, which had lost the sharpest edge ever honed a few dozen shaves ago, and a tussle with a comb made me look clean if not respectable. I tossed my towel carelessly over my shoulder and tried to whistle the music from the Andy Hardy movies. It usually made me feel better, but I couldn't remember it. Instead of the happy face of Mickey Rooney, or Lewis Stone, I kept seeing the battered face of Ralph Howard.

Gunther told me the news of the day while I had my coffee and went through a bowl of Shreddies with milk. I had to be careful with the amount of sugar I put on the spoon-sized shredded wheat since Mrs. Plaut, who might any moment come bursting into the room with some new demand, had most of my sugar ration. Closed doors did not slow Mrs. Plaut, and locked ones delayed her only a moment.

I had four bottles of Spur Cola I'd picked up a few days earlier and would have washed the toast down with one, but I didn't want to offend Gunther any more than I had to.

"I continue to be perplexed by your Li'l Abner," Gunther said, a perplexed look on his clean-shaven face. "Mammy Yokum has revealed this day in the newspaper that she has no concern for the rationing of gas for she runs her car on 'corn leavin's and strong coffee.' I do not know what these corn leavin's are, but I doubt if strong coffee could substitute for petrol."

Humor eluded Gunther. I explained the joke while I dressed in the same suit I had worn the night before. It was all I really had and I was down to my last fifteen dollars. Gunther nodded knowingly and shook his head to indicate that American humor was a continuing mystery to him.

"I will clean up the dishes, please, Toby," he said, neatly piling plates, bowls, and crumbs on his tray. I knew he preferred not to think of my less than sanitary cleaning methods. "Is there some way I can be of service in your investigation of the demise of Mr. Howard?"

"The dirty little coward who smashed our Mr. Howard," I said, tightening my tie. "When Jesse James retired he took the name of Howard, and a guy named Bob Ford shot him."

"I know of Jesse James," Gunther nodded seriously. "And what became of this Robert Ford?"

"Henry Fonda shot him in the sequel," I said. "I'll stay in touch, Gunther. Thanks for breakfast." And out I went.

Gunther would, neatly dressed, probably spend the day at his small desk translating into English from one of the six languages he knew. Gunther's business had been booming since the war, mostly with government work. My business hadn't fared as well. With war and death on a grand scale in ten countries, people were a little less interested in the home-grown one-on-one crime I dealt in.

Maybe I could stretch out my few bucks for a week or take on a retainer from Anne to help me check on Ralph's murder. I was going to do it anyway; I had a client. That reminded me. With the five from Joe Louis, I'd be up to twenty bucks, if he paid me. Who said there was no war boom in California?

When I reached the top of the stairs, it was time for my daily choice. I either ran down and tried to outdash Mrs. Plaut's curiosity, or I tiptoed in the hope that she wouldn't hear me. The latter had not worked the night before in spite of her deafness, so I chose reckless abandon. I ran like hell to the door after hurrying down the steps. No Mrs. Plaut behind, no Mrs. Plaut on the porch. The sun was blazing and neighborhood kids were in school.

I got in my car, hit the dashboard a few times in the hope of jarring the gas gauge into working, failed, and drove down Heliotrope. When I parked at No-Neck Arnie's garage, Arnie stepped out from behind a Ford hoisted on a jack in the oily rear.

"How's it going, Arnie," I said over my shoulder.

"Making a dollar a minute," he called back, which wasn't far from the truth. The war was making a lot of people rich. A thought insisted on coming forward, reminding me of the security job at Grumman Aircraft. Salary, normal hours, easy work. Jack Ellis, a hotel dick I sometimes filled in for, had told me about it, knew the guy who was hiring. But that was last-ditch stuff. At Grumman I'd have to wear a uniform. I had an allergy to uniforms. I'd worn one as a Glendale cop and as a security guard at Warner Brothers. It was no longer part of my life style. That's what I told myself when I had a hundred bucks in my frayed wallet, a few clean shirts in my closet, and a full refrigerator.

The lobby of the Farraday Building on Hoover near Ninth was, as always, clean and smelled of Lysol, which my landlord, the former wrestler and now poet Jeremy Butler, used generously, which was fine with me. I liked most strong smells: Lysol, gasoline, rubbing alcohol. They were the only ones that could get past the mashed wreckage of the cartilage in my nose.

The white tiles on the floor were worn down, a few of them showing inevitable cracks. I listened to the echo of my footsteps as I started up the fake marble stairs. There was an elevator in the Farraday, but it moved slower than a panhandler giving you change. I walked up past the floors of offices closeting bookies, disbarred lawyers, alcoholic doctors, insolvent baby photographers, some tenants whose business I didn't want to think about, at least one psychic I tried to avoid because she scared the hell out of me, and one publisher of semi-pornography named Alice Pallice. Alice was a particular friend of Jeremy Butler. She almost matched the bald giant in size and strength. She had been known to shoulder her printing press and get down the fire escape in less than a minute when the call came that vice cops were on the way.

Lately, she had begun publishing children's books and poetry with Jeremy as author. A match made in Oz.

On the fourth and final floor of the Farraday, I made my way to the door of the offices I shared with Sheldon Minck. Someone down the hall was singing an operatic aria. I couldn't tell if it was a man or woman. On the pebbled-glass door in front of me was written, in gold letters:

DR. SHELDON MINCK, DENTIST, D.D.S., S.D.
PAINLESS DENTISTRY PRACTICE SINCE 1916
TOBY PETERS
DISCREET INVESTIGATIONS

Shelly changed the sign every month or two in the hope of increasing business, but few of the people on the way to Axel the bookie down the hall were struck by whatever Shelly put on the door.

I went through the door and into the small waiting room with its two wooden chairs, a small table with a neat pile of old *Collier's,* and an ashtray. The place had been cleaned up by Shelly because of a recent investigation by the County Dental Association following a complaint about Shelly's less than sanitary technique. When I stepped through the next door I could see that the brief period of near-sterility was already passing. Dishes, cups, and instruments were beginning to peep over the rim of the sink near the door to my slightly-more-than-closet-size office. I could live with that, had lived with it for half a dozen years, but then I saw something that really got to me.

"Stop," I shouted.

Shelly turned his face toward me and away from the patient in the chair. It took Shelly a second or two to find me through his thick glasses. He was dressed in an almost white dental jacket and he held a sharp metal instrument in his pudgy right hand. With his left hand, he pushed back his slip-

ping glasses. A small bead of sweat meandered down his forehead searching for his nose.

"Toby," he said. "What the hell—"

"I think you should get out of the chair," I said, trying to
control my voice.

Joe Louis looked at me in some confusion and started to
remove the towel from his neck. Shelly turned to stop him,
but not even Shelly's determination had any effect. Louis removed the towel and stood up.

"What is this anyway?" Shelly said, looking around for
something and then seeing it. He put down the sharp instrument and replaced it with a cigar he had left smouldering on
the porcelain work table. "You don't come in and pull patients out of my office and . . ." He stopped, realizing that he
had just shoved one of my clients in his chair, and not for the
first time. Anyone who came to see me risked mutilation at
the hands of the Beast of Bad Breath.

Louis looked at both of us without expression. He had
wandered into the heavyweight warmup before the main
event. Louis was dressed in a light gray suit that looked as if it
had been pressed by a maniac who tolerated no lines. I
couldn't guess the cost, but it must have been at least ten
times that of the broken lots I picked up for ten bucks from
Hy's Clothes for Him in Hollywood.

"Mister Peters," he said, trying to work his way into the
act.

"We'll go in my office," I said, pointing to the door,
which he looked at with the knowing eyes of one who knows a
closet when he sees one. He shrugged and walked toward the
door.

"Toby . . ." Shelly said aggressively, adjusting his glasses
once more, poking his cigar in my general direction and preparing a new complaint.

"Shelly, what the hell is this 'discreet investigations' crap
on the door?" I threw in before he could attack.

He pulled his cigar back. To the ceiling he said, "See,

you do a favor for someone you thought was a friend and what thanks do you get?"

God didn't answer him, so I did. "Discreet," I said. "It sounds like . . . like . . ."

"Divorce cases," he said. "You could use some. That's where the money is in your business."

"How would you know?" I said. I opened the door for Louis and let him walk in ahead of me.

"The war," Shelly quacked behind me as I stepped in. "Infidelity, separations, broken marriages. The whole fabric of society is coming unraveled. An enterprising man sees where the . . ."

I stepped into my office and closed the door. "Sorry about that," I said. "Have a seat."

I could have said, "Have the seat," since there was only one available to him unless he took the one behind the desk, which was clearly mine. Louis sat, and I moved behind the desk and into my wooden swivel chair. Behind me, the sun came through the only window and put Louis into a shaft of light. He glanced around the room nervously. What he saw was a gray cubbyhole with two rectangles hanging on the wall. One was my dusty private investigator's license and the other a photograph of my father, my brother, me, and our dog Kaiser Wilhelm when I was nine. My father and the Kaiser were both dead. Phil and I were generally acknowledged to be alive.

Louis kept looking and I gave him a few seconds to get as close to comfortable as he could. I checked my mail and found a letter from the Rosicrucians telling me that war was raging. I knew that. They told me that their ancient teaching could help prepare for victory and peace. Another letter had a flyer telling me I could wake up my liver bile with Calomel. I wondered what would happen if I accidentally did wake up my liver bile, which must have been asleep now for at least forty years. Would it make a new man of me or clamor to get out? I played with a box of Chooz on my desk, rattled around the remaining two pieces, and then put it away.

Louis was obviously not going to start this conversation, so I reached into my pocket and came out with Ralph's photograph and notebook.

"Ever see this man?" I asked, handing Louis the photograph.

He reached over and took it. In the light from the window Louis looked young, very young. He held the photo in his right hand, a right hand that had kept him heavyweight champion for five years. He still looked like a kid sitting there.

"I seen him," Louis said. "Someone, don't remember who exactly, introduced him to me when I was working out at a place called Reed's Gym maybe a week back." He handed the photograph to me and I looked at it. Ralph was smiling slightly with his nose and all his teeth and all his hair in place.

"What did he say?"

"Nothin'," Louis said, squinting at me. "Why you asking this?"

"That's the man who got his face redecorated yesterday, the guy on the beach, the dead guy," I explained.

"I tole you," Louis said, leaning toward me. "I didn't hit him. It was those two guys."

"So, what we have here is a coincidence," I said. "You happen to be running on the beach in Santa Monica and you bump into two guys apparently killing a guy who you met a week ago."

"Something like that," Louis said with a touch of suspicion and maybe even anger on his smooth brown face. "I meet a lot of people," he went on. "Hundreds, maybe thousands. I spend as much time shaking hands as trainin'. You know?"

"I know," I said. "I'm just letting you in on what the cops are going to check if you have to talk to them."

"They'll get me good and for sure," he said, slumping

back in the chair and shaking his head. "Ain't too many people I can turn to. Marva, my wife, she ain't talking to me
much and she won't be for sure if she finds out I've been
fooling around again. My manager Roxie . . ."

"John Roxborough," I supplied. "Doing time now for a
numbers racket conviction. And your trainer . . ."

"Chappie," Louis said, looking down at his hands.

"Jack Blackburn died a few months back," I went on.
"Can I call you Joe?"

He shrugged.

"A lot of people know a lot about you," I said. "You
know that. There are people who even know Blackburn once
did time for murder. And I know the cops can tie it all together. Your choice of friends has been a little unfortunate.
Hell, you even campaigned for Willkie."

"He's a good man," Louis said, looking up as if I might
argue with him.

"I was the other guy who voted for him," I said, "but
let's not forget why we're here. You want to tell me the name
of the woman you were with last night?"

"No," he said firmly.

"I can find out," I said, folding my hands on the desk the
way Edward G. Robinson did in *Bullets or Ballots*.

"Don't find out," Louis said, standing up. "Jus' you find
out who killed that man, find out fast, and keep me out of it. I
get mixed up with this, a lot of people are gonna get hurt bad.
My mother, Marva, my brothers, sisters, people, mostly
Negro people who think I'm somethin'. This ain't the way I
wanted it. It just happened. I don't have the education and I
don't have people to help me through it now, but I mean
something to people. I wish I didn't. Lord I wish I didn't
sometimes, but you got to learn to live with what you got.
You gonna help me?"

"I'm going to help you," I said.

"Thursday, that's four days, I got to go back to Fort

Hamilton in New York. Got an exhibition for the Army. You get this all put away by then. You find who did it."

"I'll try," I sighed.

"That's all anyone can ask you," he said and stuck his hand into his back pocket. He pulled out a wallet, reached into it, and grabbed six or seven bills. "Here," he said, holding them out to me. "You need more, let me know. You can leave a message for me at the Braxton Hotel. You know where that is?"

"I know," I said, taking the money and counting it.

"My leave is over Thursday," he added, putting the wallet away.

"Hold it," I said as he turned to the door. "This is seven hundred bucks."

He stopped and reached for his wallet again. "How much more you need?" he asked.

"It's too much. Three hundred will be more than enough for a few days of work."

"Keep it all," Louis said, putting his wallet away. "You already earned most all of it last night."

He left, and I sat there looking at the seven hundred-dollar bills, the photograph of Ralph, and the black notebook.

Twenty minutes earlier I had been facing Grumman and a crap-brown uniform. Now I had more money than I'd had in years. Hell, I had more money than I'd ever had. It was tough to pull my eyes away from the cash and look at the notebook. I was tempted to let my eyes pause on the photograph for a second to thank Ralph for the windfall, but I went for the book.

It was filled with names, numbers, addresses, all printed neatly in the same hand. I imagined Ralph at a big desk in a big room with a green Waterman pen, neatly printing the name of his killer in the small book. Sure, I had no real reason to think the killer's name might be in front of me, but it was the best way I had to go. The problem was that there were too damn many names. Some were businesses, but I couldn't eliminate them. I was considering calling in help. I had the money to do it. It was something new for me, and I might have gone that way if I hadn't found something on the page of *P*s that hit me. "Parkman, Al," was nothing special. The name did tickle some memory in me, but I couldn't place it. After Parkman's name was a comma, followed by "Reed's Gym," the name of the gym where Louis had been training, where he had met Ralph. No surprise there, but why had Ralph put Louis's name in parenthesis on the next line? Not only was the name Joe Louis darkly printed, but it was underlined. Joe Louis seemed to mean a lot to Ralph Howard, though Ralph Howard apparently meant nothing to Joe Louis. Louis had said that the two men he had seen near the body looked like they had been boxers, and Anne had said that the guy who tried to run Ralph down had looked tough. Maybe it wouldn't go anywhere, but it was something to start with. I took a half hour to copy all the names, addresses, and phone numbers in Ralph's notebook. Then, as I was reaching for the phone, it rang.

"Toby Peters investigations," I said.

"Who was the nigger?" came Meara's voice.

"Let's start again, maggot mouth," I said sweetly. "You got a question? Ask it like something nearly human."

"If I were there, I'd shove a roll of toilet paper up that smart mouth of yours," he spat.

"Only an asshole like you is interested in toilet paper, Meara," I said sweetly again. "You got something to ask?"

"The nigger," he repeated.

I hung up, pocketed Ralph's notebook and photograph, and put the seven bills in my wallet after folding them neatly. The phone rang again and I considered not answering it, but I did.

"Toby Pe—" I began.

"The Negro gentleman," Meara hissed. "Who was the

Negro gentleman on the beach with you yesterday, the one standing over the goddamn body."

"What gentle—" I started, but he interrupted again, doing a lousy job of holding his temper.

"We found two kids," he said. "Two girls who live a few houses down from your former wife. They saw you. They didn't know Ralph Howard was dead. They know now. Who was he?"

"Just a guy running on the beach," I said. "He saw the body and me and asked if I needed help."

"They say he was a big guy," Meara pushed on. "Howard was messed pretty bad. And what's a ni . . . Ne-gro doing running on the beach in goddamn Santa Monica? Who runs on the beach?"

"I don't know why people run on the beach," I said, looking up at the crack in my ceiling. Today it looked like the Nile complete with tributaries.

"I want a description, Peters," Meara said.

"So you can find this man and have a nice, friendly talk with him, all about racial problems, the—"

"Peters," he said, breathing hard, "I can make your life turtle shit. You know that. I can lean on that ex-wife of yours like a Yucca tree."

"She can take it," I said nonchalantly. I didn't want him to know that he had a wedge. He'd drive it in and tear me in half.

"We might have to see," he said. "Meanwhile, I think I'll go with you as a suspect. That way we can have a friendly talk or two. I'd like that."

"I would too, Meara. You set it up with my secretary."

"You give me a name or a description or I pull you in, Peters," he shouted.

"Joe Louis," I said. "There, you pulled it out of me. It was Joe Louis. The champ was jogging down the beach and stopped to lend a hand. I feel better now getting that off my chest. You ever thought of being a Catholic priest, Meara?"

"I love jokers," Meara said, trying to pull himself together again. "I like to bend and tear them and throw them away. We don't need jokers in the deck, Peters. Nobody misses 'em."

"Depends on the game you're playing, Sergeant. Now if you'll excuse me, I've got a client."

"If you—" he started, and I hung up.

Shelly was sitting in his dental chair reading an old professional journal when I came out. The phone rang in my office but I ignored it. Shelly shook the magazine, dropped some ashes on his jacket, and shifted his pudgy body to let me know he was sulking.

"Change the sign on the door, Shel," I said. "Get rid of the discreet."

"You're not a friend," he said. "That man needed dental work."

"Shel, someday you'll think back on this and thank me," I said, going to the office door. "That man was Joe Louis. Do you know what he might do to you if you destroyed his teeth?"

"I know who it was," Shelly shot back defiantly like a small child. "And I would have given him a mouth to be proud of, a mouth that would go around the world letting everyone know, the great and the humble, that Sheldon Minck had worked on a champion. You don't get that kind of opportunity very often, Toby."

I reached into my wallet and pulled out a hundred. "You got fifty bucks, Shel?" I asked.

He looked at me over the top of his glasses with curiosity. "What if I have?" he asked cautiously.

"I'll give you a very new C-note and pay back the money I owe you and three months rent."

He scrambled out of the chair, casting his dental journal in the general direction of San Diego. It took four grunts to get his wallet out and some frantic counting to find fifty dollars. We made the exchange.

"Then I'm forgiven?" I said as he examined the bill.

"Well," he said, dragging the word out. "Yeah."

"Good, then get the sign changed while I'm gone."

And out the door I went.

On the way down the stairs I met Jeremy and Alice Pallice carrying massive cartons upward from the second floor.

"Toby," Jeremy said pausing. On his right shoulder was one large carton. Another was cradled under his left. Alice's burden was the same. "These are the covers of the book. Just delivered. Would you like to see them?"

"Sure," I said.

Jeremy put down the two cartons and reached into one of them. Alice stood smiling and waiting with her burden of what must have been a hundred and fifty pounds. I took the slick sheet of thick paper Jeremy handed me. It was dark and shiny with the title in white.

"*Doves of a Winter Night,*" I read. "Nice. I like the outline of the bird, too. How many books are you printing?"

"Three thousand," Alice said below us.

"You can sell three thousand books of poetry for children?"

Jeremy smiled and put his hand on my shoulder. If he had closed the hand, my shoulder would have been avocado pudding.

"We do not plan to sell them, Toby," he said. "We will give them away. These are dark times, Byronic times. Times swirling in the mists of world terror. I have no desire to profit from despair. These poems should, may help some children feel better about themselves and the possibility for the future."

"We have hope for the future," Alice said, looking admiringly at Jeremy.

"And what about your business?" I said to Alice.

"Oh," she said, beaming, "I'm still doing the dirty books. A woman's got to make a living and we've got thousands of servicemen gobbling up pornography all over California. Money I make on my regular stock, part of it, can go into *Doves of a Winter Night*."

Somewhere below us in the lobby a drunk who had wandered in was singing "Night and Day." Jeremy sighed deeply. "I'll take care of that when we get the covers put away," he said, picking up the boxes. "Keep the cover."

"Thanks," I said, moving down past Alice. "Good luck with the *Doves*."

When I reached the lobby, the drunk was sitting against a wall. He was as pale and skinny as any crack in the cold tile under him. He was belting out "In the roaring traffic's boom" in a not bad imitation of Fred Astaire.

"Got a tip for you, Fred," I called as I went for daylight. "Dance your way out of here before a very big man comes down those stairs and sets a new record for the javelin throw with you as the javelin."

Fred tipped his hat to me, grinned toothlessly, and didn't miss a beat as he went on with "in the silence of my lonely room, I think of you night and day."

I had been feeling pretty good coming down the stairs, but the drunk's words reminded me of Anne, and I lost some of my edge. I tucked the cover of *Doves of a Winter Night* under my arm and headed down the street for Manny's taco stand. It was early and I had downed a good-sized breakfast, but I was flush with money and a good bad meal consisting of a pair of Manny's tacos and a Pepsi would put me right again.

Two tacos and a Pepsi later I was ready for Al Parkman and Reed's Gym. I got into my Ford after telling Arnie that I wanted him to prepare for fixing the gas gauge, and I headed out toward Figueroa.

I flipped on the radio, avoided hitting an old guy crossing the street against the light, and listened to a static-broken Conga version of Felix Mendelssohn's "Spring Song" played by Xavier Cugat.

3

Reed's Gym was just where Ralph's notebook said it would be, on Figueroa near Adams. I'd passed it hundreds of times. Ralph didn't have the name quite right, however. It was REED'S SOLDIER'S GYM. The sign was old and faded. It looked as if the letters had once been gold against a green background. Now it was just letters and chipped paint. The entrance was a narrow door between an appliance store and a movie theater, the Lex, which was showing *My Gal Sal*. The theater wasn't open yet. It was only a little after one or so, but Reed's was open. I could hear the sound of men talking, grunting, swearing, laughing, above at the top of the sagging wooden stairs.

I hadn't called ahead. True, a call might have told me if Al Parkman was there, but it would also have told Al Parkman I was coming. As it turned out, Parkman was there, but first I had to get past the pug at the door.

"Ten cents," he said. He was wearing a white T-shirt that had REED'S printed on it in black. He was also wearing two of the most convoluted ears I had ever seen on a creature claiming to be a member of the human race. He really didn't say "Ten cents" either. I had to figure it out from the context and his extended hand. What he said was more like, "Tessn's."

I gave him the dime.

"Locker and towel's another dime," he said.

He was sitting on a stool, his back to the gym. When he

spoke, it looked as if he was having a bit of trouble remembering the words, which he must have said at least thirty times that day alone, judging from the sweating bodies behind him.

"No thanks. I'm just watching today." I grinned.

"You're a little old for fightin' anymore, anyway," he said, looking at me under eyelids weighted down with scar tissue.

"You got it there," I agreed. There was a ring in the far corner of the loft. Men, mostly white, were punching bags, jumping ropes, gabbing. Other guys in shirts were milling around or watching the two in the ring, who were going through the motions. Something looked wrong with the scene, but I couldn't finger it.

"You're China Rogers," I said to the battered face at the door. He did something with his face that was supposed to be a smile.

"I used to be," he said. "Ain't no more. Now I handle the door here. Know what I mean?"

"I saw you fight Packy Carl for the California middleweight title in . . ."

"September 4, 1916, Stockton," he answered. "Stopped him in the fifth with a combination. Voom, voom, right to the gut. Always went for the gut. I remember every punch I ever threw, every punch. Don't ask me what I done this morning, but every punch in eighty-three fights I could tell you, believe me."

"I believe you," I said. "Hey, is Al Parkman around today?"

"Every day," Rogers said. A kid, who looked like a Mexican about sixteen or seventeen, came up the stairs and handed Rogers two dimes and walked past me. China Rogers examined the change.

"Where is he, Parkman?" I asked.

"Back in the corner, by the ring," Rogers said. "Little guy with a mustache. Nice duds. You'll see him. But he's not taking on any fighters old as you. Needs 'em bad, but guys like us is too old."

Then it hit me. I knew what was strange about Reed's Soldier's Gym. All the boxers looked like high school kids or their fathers. The young guys were all gone, gobbled up by the Army or Navy.

"I'll see you around, China," I said.

"You really saw me fight Carl?" he asked, looking at me with a grin that showed broken teeth.

"You were great," I said.

"Went for the gut," he said as I walked away.

The strongest sensation in the room came not from the moving bodies but from the smell. Sweat and tobacco filled my nose and eyes. There were a few open windows, but they didn't help much. The closest smell I could think of was the squadroom of the Wilshire District Police Station, which had the added odor of old food and things I didn't like thinking about. I eased past a kid who looked as if he were twelve or thirteen working on a bag while a guy who looked like he was seventy yelled at him, "Faster, faster, faster." I dodged two other older guys in short sleeves, arguing their way toward the door. One guy was waving both hands and shouting, "A finiff, five. That much you can take, no more." The guy with him had his hand on the angry guy's shoulder, kneading his sweaty cotton shirt, trying to calm him.

The ring wasn't elevated. It was a floor-level mat with three strands of rope around it. The rope was covered with a badly worn material that looked like black velvet. I spotted Al Parkman with no trouble. He was standing next to a Negro with white hair. The Negro was about sixty, with strong arms and a little belly. He wore a short-sleeved blue shirt on the back of which was written *Teeth Guzman*. Parkman was about the same age as the other man, but he was pale and white with dark hair and a pencil mustache so dark it had to be dyed. He wore a suit with a gray background and thin yellow stripes. He looked like a modern painting gone all to hell. His collar was open and his tie, a red thing with some kind of animal on it, dangled over his shoulder.

"There," Parkman said to the Negro. "You see? You see? His left is down to here."

"I see," the Negro said patiently. "I tell him and tell him. I shows him and tell him some more, but that boy don't have the brain to take it in. That's the truth. He's simple."

Parkman spotted me, let his eyes run up and down my suit, and decided that he couldn't figure me out. He decided to play it without commitment.

"Josh's right," he said to me, nodding at the Negro and looking over at the two guys in the ring. "Kid's no good. Jerry in there with him was over the hill ten years ago, and if I let him go, he'd send the kid to Little Nemo land. You know?"

"I know," I said.

Josh took the opportunity of my appearance to ease away from Parkman and concentrate on his fighter in the ring.

"So," Parkman said, rubbing his nose with his thumb. "So are you fighter, promoter, or what? We're in the market for talent, but you're . . ."

". . . too old," I said. Parkman's head was bobbing up and down as we spoke, and he threw a glance at the men in the ring again.

"So, you got business, a kid, or what?"

"Or what," I said. "Ralph Howard."

Parkman stopped bouncing. A bell had rung in his head, ending the first round of our getting to know each other. Now we would start the serious jabbing.

"Ralph Howard," he repeated.

In the ring, the young fighter caught a left in the gut, and Parkman sighed.

"It's the old ones like Jerry who know to go for the gut," he said. "You wear 'em down. You think Zale or Sugar Ray Robinson go for the head? They go for the gut."

"Joe Louis," I threw in.

"Goes for the gut," Parkman said. A thin, moist line appeared on his upper lip just below the mustache.

"Let's try again," I said. "Ralph Howard and Joe Louis. What's the connection?"

"Who are you?" Parkman said, trying to find the answer in my eyes. It wasn't there.

"I represent Ralph Howard," I said.

Parkman laughed, a crackling little laugh that turned to choking.

"What's funny?"

"Nothing," Parkman said. "Nothing. The man never learns. Tell him to forget it. Better yet, I'll tell him. It can't be done."

"What can't be done?" I said.

In the ring, the young man had turned his back on the older fighter, who was standing there in exasperation, his arms down.

"Come on, son," Josh called over the gym noise.

"Just a minute here," Parkman said, hurrying over to Josh and the kid who was shaking his head. It looked to me as if the kid wasn't too simple in the head to realize that his future did not lie in the ring. I patiently looked around the room while Parkman and Josh tried to reason with the kid. After a minute or two, the kid gave in and turned to fight. Jerry, the older guy in the ring, looked over at me and gave me a well-what-are-you-going-to-do look.

"So," Parkman said, returning to me. He had a towel in his hand and was wiping his palms. "What does Howard want now?"

"Nothing," I said. "He's dead."

Parkman started to smile as if I might be joking and then realized I wasn't. "What happened to him?"

"Someone beat his face in on the beach last night," I said, watching him. It seemed to be a real surprise to him, but I've met a lot of good liars in my time.

"What the hell for?" he said. "He was good for—" Then he clammed up. "Who are you?"

"Name's Peters," I said. "I'm a friend of the Howard family. Mrs. Howard wants me to check up on her husband's business, debts, things like that."

"Well, you started with the right man," Parkman said, pointing to his own chest. "I'm sorry the man's dead but he owes me. Almost a grand. It might not be much to people like Howard, but for me it's a lot."

"For me it's a lot, too," I said. "What's your connection to Howard? Why did he have your name and Joe Louis's in his address book?"

Parkman wiped his forehead with his sopping towel and shook his head. "I'll tell you. We were trying to work out an exhibition between Louis and Teeth Guzman. Howard had a piece of Guzman, Perry, the kid in the ring, and two other fighters. Not the cream of the crop, but with what's around, you do what you can do. You catch my drift?"

"I catch it," I said. Behind us toward the door the noise level went up. It sounded like a fight and looked like it, only when I turned around it wasn't boxers going at it but the two old guys I had walked past.

"Goddamn crazy business," Parkman said. "Howard wanted to set up this fight with Louis. Even a little purse would do it, bring in enough to keep things going, and who knows, Guzman might be able to go three rounds with Louis, might even look good. Stranger things have happened, like the pyramids. You know what I'm talkin' here?"

"I get it," I said. The two old men fighting had drawn a crowd. Even the two guys in the ring had paused to see what was going on, but Josh shouted at them to get back to work.

"I think the late Mr. Howard had too much sunk into these fighters, you ask me," Parkman said.

"I'm asking you," I prompted.

"Then I'm telling. I think Howard had some partner who maybe didn't like losing money. More than that you're not getting from me. I like my knuckles the way they are, thank you, if you know what I mean."

"I know," I said. "What happened with the Louis fight?"

"Howard had some connections, friends. He got it all the way up to the damned Secretary of War, Harry Simson."

"Henry L. Stimson," I corrected.

"Whatever." Parkman shrugged, showing that he didn't give a damn. "Stimson says he doesn't want to talk about letting Louis fight while he's in the Army. Doesn't say yes. Doesn't say no. Won't talk about it is all. I guess Louis will fight Army guys but no outside stuff. Who knows?"

"Henry L. Stimson," I said.

"Seems like," Parkman agreed. "But he's not talking, not even to a big macher like Ralph Howard."

"So . . ." I pushed.

"So maybe, just maybe, and I'm not telling you this, maybe Howard's partners are not too happy with this turn of affairs. Maybe Ralph Howard made some rash promises about government connections."

The fight in the corner had stopped and everyone was back in their routine. Parkman had been close to shouting but now that the noise level had lowered, he dropped his voice with it.

"Who were Ralph Howard's partners?" I asked.

"Silent partners," Parkman said, mopping his face. "What the hell's wrong with me? What am I doing talking like this? You know what it can get me?"

"Broken knuckles?"

"If I'm lucky," said Parkman. "I don't know you. You don't know me. Take a walk, a ride. You don't want to mess with this. Tell Mrs. Howard to take the insurance and pay the bills and not look back."

"Not that easy," I said. "I'm a private investigator. If Mrs. Howard and I don't come up with the guys who killed Ralph Howard, some people are going to be in bad trouble, bad publicity for the whole fight game."

"The cops," he said, chewing on the towel.

"I think they'll be here to see you," I said. "It'll just take them a day longer than it took me. And if a cop who comes is named Meara, he won't be as nice as I am."

"I'm keeping my mouth shut," Parkman said. "I've got to learn that. You know what I mean?"

This time I didn't answer, but I did say, "Might not be a good idea to mention the Louis fight idea to the police. Get a lot of people upset."

"You kiddin'?" Parkman almost sobbed. "As of now I never heard of Joe Louis."

"You don't have to go that far. But you could give me a name, one of Howard's silent partners. I plan to talk to Mrs. Howard about paying her husband's debts. She might decide to start by paying you the grand he owed you."

Parkman was thinking and chewing on the towel.

"You want me to keep him going?" Josh called.

"No," Parkman yelled without looking at the ring.

"No goddamn good nohow," Josh sighed, stepping through the ropes.

"I gotta think about this," Parkman mumbled. "Gotta think. Come back later, tonight, make it seven. You can make it?"

"I'll be back," I said and waved at Josh.

Back at the top of the stairs, China Rogers, or the man who used to be China Rogers, put his hand on my arm. "Name a president," he said.

"Roosevelt," I said.

"Which one?" China said, puffing out his lips and rubbing his knuckles.

"Franklin Roosevelt," I said.

"Seventeen," he said instantly. His eyes met mine in triumph.

"Seventeen what?" I said.

"Seventeen letters in his name," China said. "I can do that with every president. Give me another one."

"John Quincy Ada—" I began.

"Fifteen," he said.

Across the crowded gym I could see Al Parkman looking at us. I gave China a few more presidents, told him I'd see him around, and went down the stairs. The Lex was still not open when I hit the street.

I might have been tempted by Rita Hayworth, but there was work for me to do before seven. I got in the car and headed for Wilshire Boulevard. I took it to Santa Monica and was back at the beach a few minutes after two. Paitch was coming out of the front door carrying a black leather suitcase and a why-me look. I pulled into the driveway behind the house, got out of the car fast, and cut him off.

"I got nothing to say to you, Peters, nothing," he said, trying to move past me. "I'm walking away from here, and I'm not looking back and I sure as hell ain't going to put this job on my resumé. You know that cockeyed cop and the one with the gut think I had something to do with killing Howard. Me. Can you imagine that?"

I had no trouble imagining it, since Paitch didn't look innocent. In most cases a non-innocent look was an asset in a bodyguard, but not when the bodyguard found himself a murder suspect. Actually it didn't matter how he looked. Meara was going to put his boot into everyone.

"So," he went on, "I've got nothing to say to you. I didn't know who Howard's friends were. I didn't listen in on any of his phone calls. I sat in lobbies and cars or stood across from rooms with my arms folded. Goddamn good job, let me tell you. I'd be the first to wire and pull the switch on the guy who muttoned Howard. I would. Now I gotta go."

I held out my right hand to stop him, and he put down the suitcase and placed his hands on his hips. There was a slight wind blowing from the north, and it made Paitch's windbreaker billow and snap like the sails of a small boat. His wisps of hair waved to the south like fragile pennants.

"Okay," he said. "Are we going to fight or something?

I've been up half the night with the cops. I lost my job, and now I'm going to have a fight. You mind telling me why?"

"We're not going to fight, Carl," I said. "I've only got one suit and I want to keep it clean. I want some information from you, information you maybe didn't give the cops."

His lower lip dropped enough to open his mouth. It wasn't much, but I'd been looking for it. He did have something.

"I'm willing to pay for it," I said.

"How much?" he asked, looking around to see if anyone was watching. He was one of those guys who look around when you talk about money because they can't imagine any legal way they might earn it.

"Not money," I said. "A job lead. Steady work. Security. Uniform. Good pay."

"You're not . . ."

"I'm not," I said, crossing my heart. I could have come up with twenty or more from Joe Louis's advance, but Paitch was obsessed with security.

"Okay," he said after a sigh. "Howard was in with some not very nice guys. Some people who had a piece of the same fighters Howard owned. It happens that way."

"I know that much," I said. "How about some names?"

"Names? Names? I didn't get names, but I saw him with a couple of guys I've seen around in all the wrong places. He went to that gym . . ."

"Reed's," I supplied.

"Reed's," he agreed. "And these guys were there. They talked. Looked serious. This was . . . I don't know, maybe last Thursday, Friday. But names? No."

"That's not worth a job," I said, shaking my head.

"Oh, Christ," he whispered and then inhaled salt air through his teeth. "I caught enough to figure out they were planning to fix a fight. I mean they were trying to get Howard to agree to fix a fight. A guy at the gym with loud suits and a little mustache was there. Ask him."

"Fix a fight?" I asked with doubt in my voice. "From what I hear, none of Howard's fighters went into the ring with the odds on their side."

Paitch was shaking his head, the hair settled for the moment against his freckled scalp. "No," he said. "Someone was going to fix a fight so his boy, Howard's boy, would win. A big fight Howard was supposed to set up using his Washington connections."

"And?"

"There is no 'and,'" Paitch said, picking up his suitcase. "That's all I've got. If it's not worth a job, I'll settle for cab fare. It's waiting up on the road." He nodded in the direction of the highway, where a Yellow was sitting.

"Go to Grumman, the valley plant. Tell Personnel Jack Ellis recommended you for the security job. Lie a lot about your background."

"Ellis, Grumman. Got it. Hey, you tell anybody I told you that fight-fixing business, and I say no. Got it?"

"I've got it," I said as he walked past me and hurried up the hill to the asphalt driveway.

The beach was empty when I rounded the corner of the house and looked down. Ralph's body was gone, which was no surprise, and there was no new one to replace it. There were no girls frolicking in the surf and no Joe Louis running in the sand. The sign telling frolickers to call the Marines when the Japanese invasion began was still there. When I knocked, Anne came to the door wearing a floppy green sweater and dark slacks. Her makeup was fine but her hair wasn't perfect. Almost perfect, but not perfect. She looked tired. She also looked down at the beach and licked her upper lip.

"I thought you had a maid during the day or something," I said, pulling her back from the beach.

"That Meara took Anjelica to the station to question her," Anne said softly. "Her English is awful. Anjelica is, I'm afraid, in for a very hard time."

She stepped back and I went in.

"Have you eaten?" she asked.

"Yeah," I said, following her down the hall.

"Tacos or hot dogs?" she said without looking back.

"Tuna on whole wheat, orange juice and . . . okay, tacos and a Pepsi," I finished.

Her head shook as she walked, and her low hard heels clacked against the polished wooden floor. We were in the kitchen with lots of light coming through the window and a nice view of the beach and other houses. The stretch of beach where I'd found the body wasn't visible from here. Anne poured us both coffee, and we sat across from each other at a round wooden table inlaid with Mexican tiles shaped like birds. We didn't talk for a few minutes, just drank and looked out the window.

"I called Ralph's office this morning," she said. "Ten minutes later I got a call from someone who said Howard Hughes was sorry and did I need anything. I think it was Hughes. Maybe not."

I went on saying nothing.

"Don't pursue this, Toby," she said, finally putting her cup down. "Meara will give up. Ralph's . . . he simply met the wrong people. I'm sorry if I tried to make you feel guilty last night. Ralph was responsible for himself. I don't know who killed him or why, but he's dead and I won't feel any better if they're caught."

"The cops aren't looking for the killer to make you feel better, Anne. They're doing it to make themselves feel better. I'm doing it to make myself feel better and for other reasons."

"Before you ask," she said, looking away from me to the beach, "I don't know what people Ralph was dealing with or what was going on. He was upset . . . I . . . He did have a notebook, an address book he carried with him. The police couldn't find it. It might have some names in it. They think whoever killed him took it to—"

I pulled out the notebook from my jacket pocket and held it up. She looked at it and sagged back in her chair.

"Toby. That was stupid. Leave it here. I'll tell them I found it in another jacket of Ralph's."

"Fine," I agreed. "I've copied all the names anyway. But let's take a few minutes going through it to see if anything rings a bell."

Few bells were rung by the twenty-six names in the book. The few that were familiar to Anne were social contacts and a few business ties. I made notes in my own notebook with a pencil I borrowed from Anne, and gave the social and business contacts low priority.

"And now?" she asked, getting up from the table.

"Now," I said, "we sit around and keep you company and you keep me company and we promise not to talk about old times till I have to leave. That's if you're up to a few more hours with me."

The smile was sad and a touch weary, but it was there, and deep down I thought this might be the start of something I'd given up hoping for when Anne married Ralph Howard. She took my hand and we were heading for the front of the house when the doorbell rang.

Our hands were still together when she opened it, and we found ourselves facing Meara, Belleforte, and a very frightened-looking young Mexican girl in a cloth coat. Meara smiled and looked at Anne's and my hands clasped together, then at Belleforte, who looked back at him and at us at the same time.

"This is a pleasant surprise, Peters," Meara said, clasping his hands. "This might even turn into a good day."

I didn't let go of Anne's hand.

"You've wrung all the joy out of scaring little girls, and now you want to try something more your own size. That the way it is?" I said.

Anjelica was trying to keep it all straight, but her eyes

made it clear that she understood little of what was happening.

"*Quién sabe?*" Meara said. "See, I picked up a little Mex on the job. Being a cop can be very educational. Let's you and me and Belleforte take a trip down to the station, and I'll show you our library."

"I'll pass," I said.

He shook his head no and rocked happily on his heels before he spoke. "You are coming with us now. You are a suspect in a murder. You are withholding evidence. You are a pain in the keester, Peters, and you need an education."

"I think he needs a lawyer," Anne said at my side, letting go of my hand to lead Anjelica into the house. "I'll call one as soon as you walk out of the door."

"Suits me fine," Meara said with a smile. "How's it suit you, kid?"

"Fine," said Belleforte.

"Lawyer will take maybe an hour to get back to you, go for the papers, get down to the station. Hell, our friend Peters will be lucky to be out in three hours, and by then we can get him through every book in the library. Let's go."

I turned my back on the two cops and pulled my copy of the names in the notebook out of my pocket. I pressed my list into Anne's hand, blocking Meara's view with my body.

"I'll be fine," I said. "My lawyer's name is Leib. He's in the book."

Meara's thick hand on my shoulder indicated that I was a slab of ribs and all his. Meara, Belleforte, and I left with me in the middle. I asked them to bring my car, but Meara said it would be safer right there and so we got into his black, unmarked Chrysler at the front of the driveway. I had a moment of panic, thinking the wild-eyed Belleforte might drive, but Meara got behind the wheel. I got in the back seat with Belleforte.

"You know, Peters," Meara said joyfully as he drove up

Main Street. "I've got a kid in the Army, training now in Missouri. Good kid. My wife worries about him. Hell, I worry about him too, but we pray. We wait. You know how it is?"

"I know some people in the service," I said.

It went on like that for the four miles to the station house in Santa Monica. We were almost buddies by the time we went up the four concrete steps. I was thinking of giving Meara my recipe for apple tacos.

Belleforte didn't say much, just rubbed his curly hair every once in a while like Stan Laurel. The Santa Monica station was old, but bright and sunny with lots of windows. It seemed a little sleepy on a Monday afternoon as Meara guided me to some steps leading down.

"This way," he said. I went ahead of him. "Library. You like dogs, Peters? I mean you ever have a dog?"

"I had a dog," I said at the bottom of the stairs. Meara pointed to a door. There wasn't much light from the bulb in the hall, but I could see the door. Meara touched his nose like Santa Claus in "The Night Before Christmas" and turned his left hand to show me that he wanted me to open the door. I opened the door. There was no lady, no tiger.

"My kid has a dog," Meara said, coming in behind me with Belleforte silently at his side. "Sort of like a collie."

"That's nice," I said, looking around the room. There was a wooden table, badly scarred. There were four wooden chairs, badly scarred, with one held together by rope. There was a bench running along one wall, and a small window that wouldn't have done much to brighten up the room even if there hadn't been a blue chintz curtain covering it. The only other thing in the room besides the four gray walls was a Los Angeles telephone book on the table.

"The library," Meara said, pointing at the book. "We can read or talk. Let's try talking first. Have a seat."

I had a seat. Belleforte leaned against the door with his arms folded and looked at Meara and me, though we were on different sides of the room. Meara picked up the floppy book in two hands and moved toward me.

"Heavy book, must be, what, half a million names in it? Maybe not that much. Now you got an education, Peters. Let's see how smart you are. Who was the nigger on the beach?"

"I'll wait for a lawyer," I began, and the book came down on my head. My chair screeched back an inch or two and pain shot through my skull to my chin. I didn't fall out of the chair.

"Okay," Meara said. "Let's see what you learned from the book. Books can be very educational, right?"

"Very educational," Belleforte said from the door.

I turned my head up to Meara. His face looked blurry blue in the weak window light. He was happy, a natural teacher.

"Who is he?" Meara repeated, showing me the telephone book.

"Cab Calloway," I said.

The book came down, and this time I had to reach between my legs to keep from falling.

"Who is he?" Meara repeated.

"Rochester," I said. This one didn't hurt as much. Meara was getting mad, swinging hard but not as accurately. He was getting a little old and drank too much. He was already panting from the exercise. I figured he'd tire soon. All I had to do was hold out till then.

"Who?" he said, getting the whole thing down to one word.

"Sugar Ray Robinson," I said with a grin, which made Meara wild enough to almost miss, but not quite. He caught me with the edge of the book, and the pages scraped against my right cheek like a rusty razor blade.

"You're a stubborn student," Meara panted. "Maybe you

need a special tutor. Professor Belleforte, you want to give our student a private lesson?"

"I don't think so, Sergeant," Belleforte said quietly from the door. I blinked my eyes, ran my finger across my bruised cheek, and looked at my bloody fingers and then at Belleforte, who wasn't enjoying all this. He might not be up there with Meara in the professorial ranks, but he was smart enough to stay out of this one.

"See?" Meara said, appealing to me. "See what I've got to work with? That's a partner."

"I sympathize with you," I said, trying to ignore the pulsing in my head.

Meara leaned close to me and whispered, "Has he got something to lose or something? A book doesn't leave marks. Who's in here but us?"

I showed him my bruised cheek.

"Nothing's perfect," he agreed. "I'll ask you again and then I'll hit you again. We'll keep this up till I can't hit you anymore or you tell me what I want to know. That's education. Who was he?"

"You hit me with that book again, and I go for your fat gut," I said sweetly.

"Oh," he said, putting the book down. "You touch me and you go on to the college of hard knocks. Higher education, cuffs on the wrist, and typewriters. Can you type, Peters?"

Meara, or what I could see of him through my bleary eyes, looked, to use the psychiatric phrase, a little nuts. But I'm not in the business of humoring the mentally ill.

"Can you type?" he repeated. "Let's get your clothes off, some cuffs on your wrists, and I'll go for a typewriter. How'd you like that?"

I didn't say anything, just watched the telephone book rise over his head in two blasts. I leaned to the right and caught the book on my shoulder as I threw my left hand into Meara's unprotected gut. The book splayed into the corner, and Meara staggered back against the wall, gulping for air. I got up on wobbly legs to go after him, but Belleforte said, "Don't move, Peters."

I looked at him and saw the gun. It was leveled at my chest and about six feet away. Even a cockeyed cop couldn't miss at that distance.

Meara inched his way up the wall till he was fully standing and gasped, "You . . . really are . . . a dumb son . . . of a bitch."

I got behind the wooden chair I'd been sitting in and grabbed the back. Meara tried to grin through his pain.

"Ain't we got fun," he said, his breath coming back. "Pick up that chair and so help me God I'm going to put a bullet in you. I'll aim for your kneecaps but I've just been attacked and I may not shoot straight." His gun came out of the shoulder holster, and he showed even, false teeth as he aimed.

"Sergeant," Belleforte pleaded, but Meara wasn't listening. School was out and it was my move. We listened to each other breathe for a few seconds, and I let go of the chair. Meara was taking a step toward me when Belleforte went flying across the room, his gun sailing out of his hand through the chintz curtain, through the small window, and into the afternoon.

The door had blown open behind him and a man was standing in it, a burly man with a cop gut, an angry look, and short steely hair. He wore a suit and tie, but the tie was open around his thick neck.

"Back off, Meara," my brother said.

"Get the hell out of here, Pevsner," Meara said, his gun still out. "This isn't your land."

The dazed Belleforte was on his knees, looking for his lost gun. I didn't feel like helping him.

"Meara," Phil said wearily, "you call me Captain Pevsner. Captain. And I go where I want to go, and I want to be here and I don't want to explain anything to you. Toby, you get the hell out of here."

I got the hell out of there and met my brother's former partner, Lieutenant Steve Seidman, on the stairway. Steve was a cadaverous guy who never smiled, never seemed to be disturbed by the madness of the world, and always seemed reasonable. A recently botched dental job by Shelly Minck had shown a new side of Seidman's personality, however, complete with threats to turn the myopic dentist into corn flakes.

"Hi, Steve," I said.

He nodded and looked over at the door to the library. "Anne Howard called him," Seidman explained. "I was on the way into his office. He turned me around and we got here in eighteen minutes, probably a new record."

Phil had kicked shut the library door, and we could hear his voice booming and Meara bleating back.

"He never liked Meara," Seidman explained. "They had a run-in back in about thirty-six or 'seven. Meara put Phil's name on a list of cops who used unnecessary force in getting confessions."

"There's an irony somewhere in that," I said, leaning against the wall and rubbing my head.

"Telephone book?" Seidman said, looking emotionlessly at my bloody face and handing me his handkerchief.

"L.A.," I said, putting the cloth to my tender cheek.

"Could have been worse," he countered. "Could have been Chicago or Manhattan."

Phil came out, slamming the door behind him, gave me a mean look, and pushed past me, spitting, "Come on."

Seidman and I followed him through the station and into the late afternoon.

"Get in the car," said Phil.

We got in the car. Seidman drove, and Phil sat next to me in the rear.

"Where's your car?" Phil said, looking out the window.

I told him, and Seidman headed for Anne's house.

"Thanks, Phil, I—" I began.

"I wasn't there for you," he said. "I always liked Anne. I thought she might have a chance at turning you into a human being."

"She tried," I admitted.

"You know she still sends the boys birthday presents, and the baby. She still calls . . . I did it for Anne. Besides, I hate Meara's putrid guts."

We didn't say anything for about five minutes. Phil kept looking out of the window, and I urged my senses to come back. The scrape on my cheek had stopped bleeding and screaming. The pain was down to a mild throb. I began wondering if I could make my appointment with Parkman at seven.

"Now," Phil said. "You tell me what's going on. You tell me everything. I'm not in a good mood. I have a shitload of cases on my desk and a duty roster I can't figure out. I hate that goddamn duty roster. You talk. You talk straight, or what Meara was planning for you will be party time compared to what I'll do. And you can trust me on that."

I trusted him on it. My experience told me to trust Phil when it came to violence. If my brain weren't still rattling I probably would have come up with a dangerous barb, but a wheel was loose, I was late for an appointment, and I owed him one. I talked and Phil and Steve listened. I told about Joe Louis, the guys he had seen on the beach, Parkman, everything. We were pulling into Anne's driveway when I finished.

"And that's all?" Phil said, turning to look at me. I looked at his face closely for the first time. Promotion didn't look good on him. He looked worried. The shadow of the duty roster fell over his beefy face. He had put on a few pounds he couldn't afford.

"That's it, Phil," I said.

"Get out. The case's Meara's. Stay out of his way. If something turns up, I'll reach you."

Seidman had hit the gas before I could say thanks or return his bloody handkerchief, but I knew Phil didn't want thanks and Seidman probably didn't want the handkerchief either. Phil wanted to be home with his wife and three kids, or choking an ax murderer till he confessed. What he didn't want was to go back to his office and prepare a duty roster.

I told Anne I was all right when she shuddered after getting a good look at my face. I thanked her for calling Phil, took my copy of Ralph's notebook back, and refused her offer to help me clean my face. She kissed my good cheek, and I wanted to stay when I smelled her. I had the feeling that she might let me, too, but Parkman was waiting.

I got the right time, adjusted my father's watch for no good reason, and got in the car. While I drove I listened to six student nurses beat out six members of the Des Moines Kiwanis Club on "True or False." I had just changed the station to catch a few minutes of Barbara Stanwyck and Fred MacMurray in "Ball of Fire" on the Lux Radio Theater when I found a parking space in front of Reed's Soldier's Gym. It wasn't quite dark yet and the evening was getting a little chilly.

I tried the door of Reed's, found it open, and started up the dark stairs. China Rogers wasn't on his stool and there were no sounds. The lights were out, but there was still enough of the waning sunlight coming through the windows to see there was no one in the gym.

"Parkman," I called. An echo answered.

There was a hallway at the end of the gym near the ring where Jerry and the kid had simulated battle. A dim light came from the hallway, and I went for it.

"Parkman," I called again. No answer. I came to the hall, which turned out to be a small alcove with a single door. On the frosted window of the door, stenciled in black, was PARKMAN. I knocked and Parkman's voice, scared and small, answered, "Who?"

"Me," I said.

"Who?" he repeated.

"Peters, Toby Peters."

"I don't want any. I changed my mind," he said.

"I'm not selling," I said. "I'm buying."

I tried the door but it was locked.

"Parkman, open the damned door or I'll break it. I've been beaten, threatened, and lied to, and I'm in a bad mood. Normally I'm a peaceable man like Wild Bill Elliott, but there are moments in a man's life when——"

The latch turned in the lock on the other side of the door and I could see the outline of a figure in the frosty glass. The door opened and I stood facing Parkman, wearing a frightened look on his face and the same suit he'd had on in the morning.

We were in a dark room with no windows, some desks, and a smell worse than the gym. Beyond the room was another room with a light, not much of a light but a light. The room looked like an office with a desk.

Parkman stood there, waiting for me to speak.

"Let's go in the office," I suggested.

"Let's talk here," he said. "I've got work back there, a card to put together at the Olympic for Saturday. You know how hard it is to put a card together? You line up a middleweight and he can't make the weight, or you give them a few bucks and they don't show up. They change their names, their minds, their ages. You name it, they change it. I had one——"

"Your office," I insisted.

I turned him toward the office, and he shuffled forward toward the light.

When Parkman turned on the light of the desk lamp, I knew what was wrong, had been wrong since he had told me to go away. His eyes darted to each side of the room. I couldn't see what he was looking at but I knew what was there. I decided to back away, but I didn't get the chance. A bulky figure stepped in front of Parkman.

"Just stop right there," he said. I couldn't see his face clearly, but he held himself like a fighter. Maybe I could outrun him. I turned and found myself facing another one like the guy in the room. Only this one was bigger.

"Back in the office," the new one said.

I turned and went back into Parkman's office, where a third man was sitting in the corner. I wondered if two of them might be the ones Joe Louis had met on the beach the night before.

4

The trio reminded me vaguely of the Three Stooges, a hardened king-size version dipped in bronze. The one sitting in the chair next to Parkman's desk wore a black turtleneck sweater and black pants with a gray jacket. Since he was sitting, I figured he was the brains of the three, at least what brains they had. The resemblance to Moe Howard was distant. He had the same angry look without the bangs on his forehead. Behind me stood one guy with a shaven head, though his head badly needed a new shave and soon. The tiny bristles made him look more like an angry Fuller brush than Curly Howard. The goon on the other side of me had curly hair, not as much as Larry Fine, but curly enough to allow the comparison if you ignored the scar that ran across his forehead and nose like a welt of red lightning. Turning the trio into the Stooges was designed to make it easier for me to deal with them. It didn't work.

"You wanted to see Parkman," said the one in the chair, who reminded me less and less of Moe Howard as he talked.

"Right," I said. "But I can come back later when he's not busy."

"Talk," said Moe.

"Talk," repeated Larry with the scar. He urged me on with a jab to my kidney.

"I just wanted to know if I could get a few tickets for the Saturday card at the Garden. My nephew has polio and it would . . ."

Moe was shaking his head and Parkman was trying to make himself invisible.

"No?" I asked the bulk in the chair.

"No," he said, still shaking his head. "You've been asking questions about this guy Ralph Howard's friends. Those friends don't want questions asked about them."

"One friend in particular?" I asked. Parkman was trying to signal me with his mustache to keep quiet, but I ignored him.

"Forget Howard's friends," Moe repeated.

"Someone killed Ralph Howard," I went on. "Someone who knew how to go to the face and head. Maybe a fighter or ex-fighter. You know anybody like that?"

Parkman was shaking his head furiously now, sweating and shaking.

"What's the matter with you," Moe said, pointing at me. "You dumb or something? You don't know when to shut up and walk? Or maybe you don't like walking? We can take care of that, fix you up."

"Or maybe turn my face into a jack-o'-lantern," I helped.

"What are we going to do with this guy?" Moe asked the two flanking me.

"Bust him," said Curly.

"Dance on his knuckles," mumbled Larry with the scar. I turned to look at him. You've got to admire creativity even in a situation like this.

Moe sat thinking, and Parkman sat shrinking, and I looked around at the walls while I tried to think of what to do before they took one of their alternatives. The walls were covered with dirty wall paper, vertical blue stripes on a light blue background. Between the stripes were shapes that looked like Chinese lanterns, dark blue Chinese lanterns. Pictures were all over the place, photographs of boxers. Some of them were facing the camera with their fists up, wearing grins or serious grimaces. Some had arms draped over guys I didn't recognize.

A few, like Gus Lesnevich, had an arm draped over the shoulder of Al Parkman, a younger version with a grin.

"That Billy Conn?" I asked Parkman, pointing to a photograph on the wall I knew was Billy Conn. I took a step toward the one source of light in the room, the lamp on Parkman's desk.

"That's Conn," Parkman said without enthusiasm.

"He's in the Army now, isn't he?" I said.

"Yeah," sighed Parkman, touching his little mustache to be sure it was still there. He had trouble finding it. "Yeah, a private," he said. "He's in the hospital now. Fractured left hand."

My hand was on the desk as I stood admiring the photograph and gauging where the three pugs were in the room. The space between the two at the door wasn't much, but it was possible.

"Who did he fight?" I asked.

"His father-in-law, at home with his father-in-law. Can you live with that?" Parkman said, warming to the conversation a little.

"Peters," Moe said, getting out of the chair. He had made a decision. "You don't ask no more questions, not around here, not about fights, not about Howard. We're going to mess you around a little, not too bad, enough to remind you, and then you're going to crawl away and not bother anybody again. You understand?"

"I understand," I said. "Can I get in one last question before we dance?"

Standing up he was a lot bigger than I had imagined. My guess was six-four. He was a few inches from me. I could smell his dinner on his breath, which reminded me that I hadn't eaten and helped me not to want to think about it.

"There's no being nice to some people," Moe said.

"Two guys were seen walking away from Howard's body on the beach at Santa Monica, two guys who looked like they might be in the game. And another guy, maybe one of the two, tried to run down Ralph Howard last Saturday. You wouldn't know who these guys might be, would you?"

Moe looked puzzled and moved his eyes past me to Curly and Larry, questioning. It was time. My stomach grumbled and I hesitated. My head was still vibrating like a tuning fork from Meara's game with my head, and my face was raw. I knew a session with these guys would land me in a hospital. On the other hand, if I did what I was planning and I didn't make it, I could wind up a corpse with $650 in my pocket, down for the final count. What the hell. You only live once or twice. I reached past Moe, grabbed the lamp, and threw it in the corner of the room. The cord snapped and the room went dark.

I turned and ran toward the space between the two at the door, my hands out like Bronco Nagurski. I hit one of them, felt the other grab at my sleeve in the dark, pulled away, and stumbled into the outer office.

"Grab that bastard," Moe hissed. "Get the damn light on."

I tripped over something and fell on my knee, got up and reached for the door. It wasn't locked. I threw it open, took a deep breath and a chance. I didn't go out into the gym. I wasn't sure I could make it if I did. The run was long, ending with a flight of steep stairs, and they might have guns. My .38 was in the glove compartment of my car. I almost never carried it, and rarely shot it. When I did, I almost always missed what I was shooting at.

I scrambled into a corner, trying to find the desk I remembered being there. My head found it, and I bit my tongue to keep from groaning. There was plenty of noise behind me where the Stooges were running into each other trying to find a light. One of them groped his way into the outer office, found a desk lamp, and switched it on. I didn't see which of them did the switching. I was behind the desk, trying to turn myself into a medicine ball.

"Go on, go on, go on," Moe said, and their footsteps told me that they had gone through the door and into the gym.

"Find the damn lights," Moe shouted. "Mush, get to the stairs. Don't let him get out."

They ran, calling to each other, searching, and I crawled out from behind the desk and made my way as quietly as I could back to Parkman's office. I moved past the door to his inner office and to the left into the darkness away from the dim lamp light from the outer office. "He's somewhere," shouted Moe. "Check the locker room, behind those mats, move stuff. Get moving. I want that shit's heart."

They sounded as if they had moved across the gym, away from the office. Since they weren't high on the list of people likely to make a bundle on "Information Please," I figured it would take them three or four minutes to come back and check the office. Tops, I had five minutes till they decided to come back and push Parkman around a little more.

"Parkman," I whispered.

"Uggh," Parkman gasped. He was in the dim shaft of light from the lamp and looked as if he had just had a rope pulled around his neck.

"Shut up," I whispered. "I've got to get the hell out of here. Does that window open?"

"It opens," he whispered.

"Where does it lead?"

"Little roof, then a fire escape next to the movie. Move, get the hell out of here before they come back and redecorate my walls with both of us."

"Who do they work for, Al?" I said, standing and looking back toward the gym. Larry darted past the door on the other side of the far room.

"Didn't you hear for chrissake what they said? No questions?"

"Who sent them?" I repeated. "Who was Howard's partner?"

"Lipparini, Monty Lipparini. There, you satisfied? You

know what that information is going to get you? Get me?
Now get out, get out, get out."

Parkman's voice had risen with each "get out." He was
still whispering, but loud enough for the sound to carry out to
the gym.

Someone was running across the gym, toward Parkman's
office. I went to the window behind him and pulled. Nothing.
I pulled again and realized it was locked. I shoved the dirty
shade out of the way, not worrying any more about the noise,
and pushed the metal latch with my thumb. Then I pulled the
window open. The metal handle came off in my hand with
two screws dangling. I threw it aside as the footsteps pounded
behind me, entering the outer office.

I ducked my head and went through the window into
darkness hoping that Parkman was right about the roof and
that I wouldn't fall two floors into an alley. My feet touched
the gravel-covered roof. I looked around in the dim light from
the stars and the shops and stores on Figueroa and went for
the curled metal of the fire escape over the edge of the narrow
roof. I slipped on the pebbled surface as a familiar and not
welcome sound cracked behind me.

"Hold it there you bastard," Moe shouted. I could see no
advantage in stopping right there for him to take a shot at a
non-moving target, so I scrambled over the edge of the roof
and down the ladder. I could hear him coming through the
window after me. Without jumping, I could see no way of
making it to the alley before he leaned over the fire escape
and leveled his gun at me. The alley wasn't well lit, but it was
bright enough for Moe to see the garbage cans and the street
and me.

About five feet down I found a window and pushed at it.
It opened, and I went through head first into the darkness and
scuttered down the wall to a floor. Behind me, the shadow of
Moe fell across the window, and I got up. The window had
been small. I'd just made it through, and there was a chance
Moe wouldn't fit, but I wasn't taking that chance.

A light switch would have been nice if I were willing to turn on the lights so Moe could get that clear shot at me, but darkness was better. I felt along the wall, cracking my shin on something low, brushing my already scraped face on something metal, probably a shelf. And then I found the door. I didn't stop to look back to see how the grunting pug behind me was doing. I closed the door behind me and found myself in a narrow corridor lit by a small bulb with a metal reflector. The walls were covered with movie posters going back to *Bronco Billy and the Girl.* I hurried past *Hearts of the World, Dick Turpin,* and *Underworld.* About halfway down the hall Rita Hayworth said, "Wait a minute."

I turned, expecting to see Moe doing a comedy act that I'd just have time to applaud before he shot me, but he wasn't there. I could hear him still struggling in the room I'd come out of. Then Rita Hayworth spoke again, and I realized that I was somewhere in the Lex Theater, next door to Reed's. *My Gal Sal* was all around me. I turned again and went through the door, found myself on a narrow metal stairway, and went down in darkness to another door. Beyond this door, Rita Hayworth's voice called to me. I stepped in and found myself in the theater looking up at Victor Mature's teeth. His forehead wrinkled at me, and I moved up the aisle toward the exit. There were a few people in the theater who paid no attention, but a spindly guy with a bow tie stepped in front of me when I hit the lobby.

"I don't remember your purchasing a ticket," he said.

"I came in with the fat lady," I answered. "My aunt. I was just getting up to get some popcorn when I slipped on something wet on the floor. Fell down and scraped my face. Look at this." I pointed to my bruised cheek. "I may need stitches," I said. "I may sue you."

"It's not our fault if a customer spills—" he began, now on the defensive.

"I don't care," I said. "I don't want to sue you. I just want to get to a doctor. But since you bring it up, there is a big man in there, a tough-looking ape who went into a door near the stage. He didn't look like anyone I've seen working here."

"Door near the—" he began.

"Can't miss him," I said, moving away through the lobby, past the candy counter toward the exit. I stopped outside the theater on the street, standing in the sputtering light of the remaining bulbs in the Lex's sign. Larry and Curly weren't waiting outside of Reed's. I turned left, walking fast, looked back over my shoulder, and crossed the street at the corner. Then I worked my way back to hide in a doorway and watch the front of Reed's. From the darkness of the doorway, I saw Moe come out of the Lex, shaking off the spindly guy with the bow tie. Moe looked up and down the street, didn't see what he was looking for, yelled "Shit," and went through the door to Reed's. I made my way fast to a Rexall's on the corner and found the pay phone and the Los Angeles book. Reed's was listed.

I dropped my nickel and dialed the number. It rang six times before Parkman answered, his voice cracking, "Yes?"

"Put the ape on the phone," I said. "The lead singer."

"It's for you," Parkman said, and Moe came on.

"Yeah?"

"I just called the cops," I said. "They should be there in a minute or two. It might be a good idea if Parkman's in one piece when they get there."

"I'm gonna find you, you piece of—" he started.

"I'm not hard to find if you can read a phone book," I said. "Which means I'm safe from you at least till you get through second grade." I hung up.

I figured the Stooges would go for their car and get the hell out of there. I went to the luncheonette counter in the drugstore, sat on a red leatherette-covered stool near the window, and hid behind a menu, watching Reed's door.

"What'll you have?" asked the waitress, who seemed to be full of uniformed good cheer. She was pudgy, pink, and not very busy. I ordered the lamb stew with vegetables for twenty-two cents with a nickel order of cole slaw and a Pepsi.

"I might have some pie later," I said, to explain why I held onto the menu.

"Take all night," she said. "I'm on till we close."

The Stooges came out of the door to Reed's just as she turned away with my order. They didn't look around, just went for a dark sedan that happened to be parked right behind my car in front of Reed's. They drove away, burning rationed rubber, and I put the menu down. Parkman came through the door of the gym, turned and locked it, looked around the street to see what new surprises were in store for him, shuddered, and hurried away into the night.

I finished my dinner and, at the happy waitress's suggestion, took on a slice of blueberry pie.

"You want some advice," she said as she watched her lone customer eat.

"I want some advice," I said.

"Take care of that face. Looks like it could get infected or something."

I finished up, bought some peroxide and cotton, and headed for my car.

On the way home I thought about Monty Lipparini. I knew the name but not the man. He had moved West about ten years ago from Philadelphia, supposedly a mob front man. Lipparini made the papers every once in a while, showed up at fights, made donations to charity, and never let anyone know what he had his hands into except for his automobile dealership. That he had a piece of various fighters didn't surprise me. It didn't even surprise me that he had found a way to get Ralph Howard to front for him, but it didn't make sense that he would have Ralph killed rather than work on Ralph to pay him whatever he owed, if he owed.

"You can't collect from a dead man," Lipparini had told a reporter once, and the quote had been picked up and repeated on the street—the businessman's creed, only sometimes someone got a little antsy and there was a dead man.

The next step, after a good night's sleep, was to find Lipparini or let him find me. With my cotton and peroxide at my side, I drove back to Hollywood, listening to the radio.

Gas rationing, I found, was here. That was the bad news. The good news, according to the Blue Network, was that the RAF had hit the Krupp plant in Essen with 1,036 planes. The other bad news, at least for Charlie Chaplin, was that Paulette Goddard had divorced him in Mexico. That was enough news. I turned the dial to the "Battle of the Sexes." Four male and four female doctors were trading insults. I didn't listen long enough to find out who won.

Mrs. Plaut and I had a brief but fruitful chat in which I discovered that no one had called me, that I was expected to turn over one-third of my gas rationing allotment when it came, and that I had a very bad bruise on my cheek. My conversation with Gunther was more pleasant. He was translating John Steinbeck's new book, *The Moon is Down*, into Norwegian. He guessed that the government planned to sneak copies into Norway to undermine the Nazis and give moral support to the resistance. I listened while I finished off one of my bottles of Spur. In consideration of Gunther, I drank it from my Porky Pig glass rather than from the bottle.

After I worked on my face in the bathroom down the hall and downed a handful of aspirin for my head, I went back to my room and told Gunther what had happened, how I got the bruise, and what I planned to do.

"Of course," he said, "I will be most happy to be of assistance in any way I can possibly be of such assistance."

I thought of a way and offered to pay him for his help, but he was offended.

"I need no money, Toby," he said. "It satisfies to feel that my service can aid in a worthwhile cause. I should not like to see the image of Mr. Joseph Louis affected, and I should like in some way to possibly contribute to finding these killers and putting to rest your former spouse's concerns in this matter."

I thanked him and suggested that he track down Parkman, follow him, keep an eye on him, and let me know if the Three Stooges showed up. Gunther agreed with enthusiasm. I knew he would be on it by dawn, that he would stay in his car with the special built-up pedals a discreet distance behind Parkman at all times. I advised him not to go into Reed's, just to watch the door. A midget in a gym might be too easy to spot. There was no sixty-five-pound category.

When Gunther left my room around midnight, I wound my watch and wondered if it was too late to call Carmen the cashier at Levy's restaurant on Spring. She would be getting off in twenty minutes. My blood was up and I didn't feel like sleeping. I actually started toward the door to the hall with nickel in my hand. Then I stopped. Something made me feel that a call to Carmen would betray Anne. It was stupid. Anne had promised me nothing, given me no opening, no real hope. She needed a friend. That was all. I should do what I could for her and get back to my own life. She would. Anne always bounced back. I put the nickel back in my pocket, took off my suit, and sat at my table for another hour working on Mrs. Plaut's manuscript. I read to the end of the chapter and found that:

Uncle Machen urged the crazy man known as Kyle to accompany him to the mine, but Kyle, who was crazy but not stupid, declined and said that he would rather return to Walter's Lump and live out his days as a bachelor, to which Uncle Machen said, "Bunk."

It was then that Uncle Machen ventured into the mine once again in search of God-knows-what, gold and his brother Albert, who may himself have disappeared in the mine the year before.

The ways of the Lord and the Doyle family are various and, I am sorry to say, sometimes wicked. Uncle Albert turned up in Juarez some months later, living with a Mexican family engaged in manufacturing cigars of an inferior nature. In the meanwhile, Uncle Machen had entered the mine never to be seen again. I say never to be seen because it was claimed that he was frequently heard, him or his ghost, singing "Lead Kindly Light" or a bawdy ballad learned in his days as a cleanup boy in the Red Water saloon of New Orleans.

Such are the travails of the Doyle family.

Such are the travails, I agreed, putting the manuscript aside and heading for my mattress. Sleeping proved to be a dilemma. I had to stay on my left side to keep my bruised face from touching the pillow. I think it took me all of ten minutes to fall asleep.

5

After placing Mrs. Plaut's chapter gently and quietly in front of her door in the morning, I hurried to my car and drove downtown. I told Arnie the no-neck mechanic to fix the gas gauge and hurried to the office.

The lobby was empty, the building was echoing and humming, and my cheek was puffy and tender, but I felt good. Even with the twenty bucks Arnie would gouge from me for fixing the gauge I was still well over six hundred bucks. I considered going to the bank and opening an account. It would be the first one I'd had since Anne and I had been married. There had never been much in that account, at least not much that I supplied.

Shelly had taken the word DISCREET off of the door, but he hadn't bothered to center the remaining INVESTIGATIONS, so the word sat off to the right under my name, looking as if it were about to fall off the window. Shelly was at work on a patient when I came in. I couldn't see who he was, but Shelly was strangely silent. With a victim in the chair, Sheldon Minck normally babbled, sang, or hummed away.

"Any messages, Shel?" I asked.

He grunted something that sounded negative and stood back from his patient. In the chair sat Lt. Steve Seidman, his mouth open, a white towel around his neck, and a pistol in his lap.

Shelly looked at me, pleading, his scalp covered with sweat.

"Hi, Steve," I said. Seidman nodded, his face more pale than usual.

Shelly was mouthing something to me, trying to conceal his mime from his patient.

"What are you trying to say, Shel?" I asked.

"He's going to shoot me," Shelly whispered, his voice dry. He grabbed at his glasses just as they were about to clatter to the floor. "He's going to shoot me if I don't fix his teeth right."

"Sounds reasonable to me," I said.

"That's not funny, Toby," Shelly said, moving toward me, a thin, pointed instrument in his hand. "You've got to help me. Reason with him for God's sake."

"Okay, Shel," I said, backing away before he could put a sweaty hand on my no longer new suit. I had brushed it off, but it had picked up dirt from Reed's gym and the roof outside Parkman's window and several trips, spills, and plunges in the night. I needed a change of clothes and resolved to put out a few dollars of Joe Louis's money. "Steve, are you planning to shoot Sheldon if he messes up your teeth again?"

Seidman nodded affirmatively.

"He wouldn't do that," Shelly said, looking back at Seidman. "He's a policeman. He wouldn't shoot someone, a fellow professional, for an honest human error."

"I don't know, Shel," I said, moving to my door. "He might. And I don't think performing oral surgery without a certificate falls under the heading of honest human mistakes."

Shelly held his hands up to the sky. "What would my father say if he could see this, see what his son is surrounded by?"

"I don't know, Shel," I said sympathetically. "Why don't we call him and ask him. But didn't you tell me once he wouldn't talk to you after you cleaned his teeth in 'sixteen?"

"I was just starting out then," Shelly said. "Aren't you going to help me anymore? Is that all you have to say?"

"No, I think you'd better get back to work on Lieutenant Seidman and be very, very careful."

Seidman was tapping the barrel of his gun against the arm of the chair to attract Shelly's attention. Shelly turned with resignation back to his patient, and I went into my office, pausing to rinse a white cup that had *Welcome to Juarez* written on it and pour coffee from the pot near the sink.

There was no mail on my desk. I placed my Juarez coffee cup down, watched the steam curl from it for a second or two, and pulled out the list of names I had copied from Ralph's notebook. I also took out my wallet, removed five hundred dollars, and put it in my lower desk drawer, in the pages of a hard-cover copy of *The Collected Poetry of William Blake*. Jeremy had given me the book for my birthday a year ago. I'd never read it, and I couldn't imagine anyone who might come into my office reading it, at least not the people who might come into my office and go through the drawers.

Lipparini's name wasn't on Ralph's list, but there was an M. L. Automobile Sales in North Hollywood. I hadn't thought about it when I had first looked at it; it just seemed like a place where Howard might have picked up a Lincoln or a big Packard. Now the name made sense. I dug out the nickel I had planned on using the night before to call Carmen, dropped it into my pay phone, and dialed the number.

"M. L. Auto," a woman's voice chirped.

"I'd like to talk to M. L.," I said.

"I'm sorry," she said, sounding as if it was the saddest duty she might have in a lifetime, "but there is no M. L. Would you like to speak to our sales or service manager?"

"No," I said, "I want the finance manager, the boss, Mr. Lipparini."

"Whom shall I say is calling?" she asked after a pause.

"Toby Peters," I said.

"I don't think he is in right now, Mr. Peters," she said.

"Tell him it's the guy who danced with his stooges last night."

I played with the tip of a pencil, trying to scratch it into a point I could use while I waited. I didn't have to wait long.

"Peters?" The voice was deep, the name said languidly.

"Right," I said.

"You're dead," he said.

"You want to hear a corpse talk?" I answered.

There was no sound on the other side, but the line stayed open. He didn't hang up. So, I continued.

"I've been through Ralph Howard's papers," I lied magnificently, "and I have evidence that you and he were involved in a deal to fix some fights, that you owned a piece of the fighters Howard supposedly owned on his own. I'm putting things together and I find the possibility that Howard made you unhappy, maybe he couldn't fix the contracts, or set up an exhibition with Joe Louis, or pay back some money he owed you fast enough, or . . . It can go on. But suddenly the day before yesterday Howard meets two guys who look suspiciously like a pair of the walking radios you had at Reed's last night. And Howard is now dead. It wouldn't look good for you if people I know at the L.A. *Times* got this."

"You can't . . ." he began.

"Collect from a dead man," we finished in unison, and I went on alone to say, "I know the line. Something happens to me and the envelope of Ralph Howard's letters and business dealings with you gets mailed to the district attorney by a friend of mine."

"No one's going to hurt you," he said, taking forever to say it. "You upset Jerry a little last night. He'll get over it."

"And?" I said, pleased that I was no longer a dead man.

"And," he went on, "I didn't have Howard killed. He owed me, yes, he owed me. Maybe I juiced him a little, had someone chase him around in a car on a Saturday night, a nice new Pontiac maybe, but I didn't have him killed. You know my motto."

"Engraved on my cheek," I said. "Let's talk."

"We're talking," he said. "But you talk about me paying you for those Howard papers and we stop talking. I don't go in anybody's pocket."

"No money," I said, turning my chair around with a rusty squeal to look out the window. "Information. You think it's possible a pair of your boys might have gotten overly enthusiastic about their job, accidentally did Ralph Howard in, and then decided not to take the responsibility?"

"No," he said simply, and then after a long pause: "They do what I say, no more, no less, or they have a long swim in the ocean."

"I'd like to talk to that trio from last night," I said. "You name the place and I'll be there."

I thought he had gone out for a hot dog. There was nothing on the line for a minute or two and then he said, "Here, half an hour. Come alone. I'll give you ten minutes, and then I don't want to hear from you or see you again ever."

"Half an hour," I said and hung up.

I was five minutes late. No-Neck Arnie had just been putting the finishing touches on my new gas gauge and I had to wait.

"Putting one of those things in ain't easy," he said, wiping his hand and holding it out for payment.

"It ain't cheap either," I answered, shelling out two tens and two singles.

The gauge worked fine. Arnie had thrown in a full tank of gas and a warning about rationing, which led me to believe that the cost of running my car would be going up.

M. L. Auto was on Sherman Way just off of Laurel Canyon Drive. It was big and bright with lots of windows and three rows of used cars in the outside lot. The lot and the showroom didn't seem to be overrun with customers. Two guys who looked like salesmen looked at me when I came through the front door. Then they glanced at each other to see who would get me. Neither seemed eager for the possible sale. Finally, the shorter of the two put his left hand in the pocket of his nicely pressed trousers, touched his bow tie, and ambled toward me past a shiny '38 Oldsmobile. He wasn't young and he wasn't full of car salesman energy. His black hair was brushed back and he had nice heavy bags under his eyes.

"Hi," he said, holding his hand out.

"Hi," I returned, shaking his hand.

"My name is Jerry," he went on. "We've got nothing new. Won't be anything new till the war ends, but we have some good-as-new pre-war models, fully reconditioned, real rubber tires."

"I'm here to see Mr. Lipparini," I said. "I've got an appointment and I'm late."

Jerry hadn't been smiling, and he not-smiled even more and took his hand out of his pocket with a bit of respect. "Up the stairs, first door," he said, pointing to a carpeted flight of wooden stairs against the wall. He returned to his fellow salesman in the corner.

I found the door at the top of the stairs, knocked, and a woman's voice told me to come in. The office was carpeted, with wood-paneled walls, pictures of cars, cozy. The blonde behind the desk looked cozy and warm, too. She was about twenty, had on a businesslike green dress and a nice smile, showing white teeth. Leaning against the wall behind her was my old friend Moe. He had changed suits but not dispositions. His arms were folded, but his eyes were aimed at me, which wasn't too bad. It was the little smile I didn't like.

"Mr. Peters?" the blonde said.

"He's Peters," Moe confirmed. She looked at Moe and then back at me, still smiling.

"Mr. Lipparini has been expecting you," she went on. "Just knock and go right in."

I knocked and went right in.

Lipparini was seated behind a big black desk. No trouble recognizing him. I knew him from his pictures in the papers.

The happy grin under a small nose. The thinning hair combed sideways to make it look like more, but instead making him look like a man who was trying to fool himself. He was about sixty and in reasonably good shape. His gray eyes looked like they belonged in a different face, or else the real Monty Lipparini was wearing a mask and only his real eyes were visible. I didn't want that mask to come off. I had the feeling that people who saw the real face turned to stone or worse.

"Peters," he said, shaking his head. "Hell of a world. Hell of a world."

"Hell of a world, Mr. Lipparini," I agreed, though it didn't look like such a bad world for him. I tried to ignore Curly and Larry standing to the right of the desk. Larry's scar looked fleshy and his face puffy, like a little kid who's just been caught going through the pockets in the coat room.

"I just heard on the radio the Japs bombed some place called Dutch Harbor in Alaska. Nineteen planes. That's the first raid on the United States." He looked genuinely concerned, at least his face did. His eyes were watching me.

"Pearl Harbor," I said.

"Right," he agreed, standing up and plunging his hands in his pockets. He was wearing a shirt and tie but no jacket. His sleeves were rolled up and ready for work. His arms were dark and hairy. "I mean the first attack on the coast, the continent, America, not some island a million miles away. They hit Alaska and then they hit Seattle or Frisco or Los Angeles. You know what would happen? You remember what happened in February?"

He looked at me and I nodded. The air-raid sirens had gone off about two o'clock in the morning. I had rolled out of bed to check the windows, and when I saw searchlights aiming into the sky, I'd gone downstairs to join the other tenants of Mrs. Plaut's boarding house. We stood and watched without knowing what was going on. Far away someone was pumping ack-ack rounds at the moon, and an air-raid warden came running down Heliotrope holding his metal pot on his head with one hand and telling us to go in and turn out the lights. It went on like that for two hours, till the sun came up. The next morning the L.A. *Times* told us foreign bombers had raided Southern California. There was even a report that a plane had been shot down near 185th and Vermont. It turned out that no planes had flown over California or been shot down, though there were casualties. Three people were killed in car crashes when they tried to get out of the city to avoid the oncoming Japanese. Two others had heart attacks. Air-raid wardens went down non-fatally all over the place after running into walls or civilians. The ack-ack had destroyed roofs, lawns, cars, and a Chinese restaurant.

"Christ." Lipparini went on pacing behind his desk. "If the Japs really came . . . You want coffee or something?"

"No thanks," I said. Curly and Larry didn't say anything.

"I'm trying to be a little friendly here," Lipparini said. "You called me pushing and I'm trying to make it a little friendly."

"Coffee would be great," I said.

"Okay, that's better." He picked up one of the two phones on his desk, pushed a button, and said, "Mr. Peters would like a coffee. . . . I don't know. Give him cream and sugar." He hung up, still standing, gave the two standing men a disgruntled look, and turned his attention back to me.

"I didn't have Howard killed," he said. "I didn't even have him worked on. I was thinking about it, but I didn't. And my boys didn't do it on their own."

He looked at Curly and Larry, who didn't look back.

"If I found out they did, they'd be swimming for Japan."

"I thought you didn't get rid of people," I said.

"I said," he corrected, "I don't get rid of people who owe me. If my people spin on me, they owe their skins, and the only way I can collect it is if I take it from their bodies."

It was a pleasant image but I didn't want to dwell on it. I might owe my skin to Monty Lipparini some day. I considered not going on, saying good-bye, and searching for a new suspect. The light might not be as good on the street, but it would be a lot safer. There was a knock at the door and the bouncy blonde came in, smiling at all concerned, and handed me a cup of coffee. I took it, said thanks, and she left. Lipparini watched me. Curly and Larry watched me. I drank some coffee and smiled appreciatively. It was too sweet.

"How you like it?" Lipparini asked, cocking his head as if my answer was very, very important.

"Good coffee," I said, taking another sip. The answer was right. It widened Lipparini's grin and he pointed to the empty chair in front of his desk. I sat down.

"I'm going into the coffee business," he said. "Cars are too damn much trouble during a war. I'll keep this place going but what the hell, you can't get parts, tires, gas, cars. But coffee, that I can get. I've got a source in Cuba. What you're drinking there is M. L. coffee. I got a couple of guys working on an ad for the radio. We're going to be on the Milton Berle Show. M. L. coffee, one sip will make the war seem far away. How do you like it?"

"Great," I said.

He was around the desk now, leaning close to me. It was hard to get the cup to my mouth. He looked at me for a few seconds and backed away. "What happened to your face?"

"A cop shoved me," I said.

Lipparini nodded knowingly. He had been shoved by cops. "The way I figure it," he said, "the only one who figured to gain from this Ralph Howard's getting it is Howard's widow. How about that?"

"She didn't do it," I said, putting the empty cup down on the desk. Lipparini nodded and Silvio, who I had thought of as Larry, leaped forward to pick up the cup and wipe the ring I had left with his pocket handkerchief.

"Parkman," Lipparini said, holding up a finger.

"Why?" I asked.

"Howard owed him. I don't kill people who owe me but that doesn't mean other people have my ethics."

I wasn't getting far this way. All I was getting was cheap coffee and weak ideas.

"How were you going to fix the fight with Louis and Teeth Guzman?" I asked.

To my right Curly, who I now knew was Mush, sucked in his breath. Lipparini stood back and looked at me as if I were insane. His smile left for a second and came back.

"You're a crazy man," he said.

"Humor me." I grinned.

"You know boxing?" he said. "More coffee?"

"I know boxing," I answered. "No more coffee."

"Ever see Louis fight?"

"Roper, 1939," I said. "Louis put him away in the first."

"Okay," said Lipparini. "But first Roper tagged Louis with a left, hurt him. And Galento. I saw that one. Galento went down in the fourth, but he had Louis down. See what I mean? Some bum of the month could get lucky."

"Or," I contributed, "some bum of the month could be helped to get lucky."

Lipparini shrugged, indicating that it was possible, and said, "Something in Louis's water. Or maybe someone could talk to him about life insurance for his wife or his sisters or his mother. People do things like that, Peters. Sure you don't want another cup?"

"I'm sure. Yeah, I know people do things like that. Hell of a world."

"Now you got it." He grinned. "I told you that when you walked through that door. Just took you a while to soak it in. You can go now. It's been good talking to you, but I don't want to see you or hear from you again. If I have to I can handle that file you say you've got on me and Howard. I'll look bad, have a little trouble with the boxing commission, a little chat from some partners back East, but I can live with that if I really want your skin."

I got up and went to the door. "Thanks for the coffee," I said. "Made the war seem far away."

Moe was still standing in the same place in the outer of-fice. The blonde was on the phone, listening and nodding her head. I grinned at him and went out.

When I got to my car, I remembered what Jack Roper had told the reporters after Louis put him away. "I zigged when I should have zagged," Roper had said. I knew the feel-ing. I stopped for a pair of cheeseburgers and a Victory shake at a stand on Laurel Canyon. The Victory shake tasted like plain vanilla to me, but it was served in a red, white, and blue plastic cup.

I drove through the hills on Laurel Canyon and then went over to Figueroa. The picture at the Lex had been changed. Today's feature was *The Elephant Boy* with Sabu. I found a space a half-block away from the entrance to Reed's, not far from the Rexall's where I had eaten the night before. I got out and looked around. Gunther was parked directly across from the Reed's entrance. I got into his car from the passenger side.

"How's he doing, Gunther?" I asked.

"He is a nervous man, Toby," Gunther said. His head barely made it over the window ledge. More than one driver passing Gunther on the road must have thought he was seeing a driverless car. "He arrived here at eight thirty-four and has come outside four times looking both ways as if he expects someone who has not arrived."

"Can you keep on him for a few more hours?" I asked.

"As long as you see fit," he said seriously.

"Thanks," I said. "How about we take in a restaurant of your choice on my client when this case is over?"

"That would be very nice," Gunther said.

I got out, closed the door, waited for a truck to pass, and crossed the street to Reed's. China Rogers was at his post.

"Teddy Roosevelt," I said, coming to the top of the stairs. China was wearing a blue pullover today.

"Theodore," he said, beaming. "He's seventeen."

"Alexander Hamilton," I returned.

"Seventeen, but he wasn't a president," China said seriously. "But Franklin Roosevelt's a seventeen, too. Lot's of seventeens, if you don't count middle names."

I plunked a dime into China's gnarled hand and stepped into the sea of bodies banging, running, jumping, grunting, throwing, and catching in the gym. I spotted Josh the trainer in the corner by the ring, but no Parkman. I made my way ringside to Josh, who stood with his arms folded, a white towel draped over the shoulder of his gray sweatshirt.

"The right," he shouted. "The right."

The guys in the ring were bigger than the ones yesterday. One was slightly taller than the other, very black and fast. The other was a little smaller, slower and more tired. His face was red.

"Hi," I said, stepping next to Josh. He nodded to me.

"More of Parkman's boys?" I said, looking at the two men puffing in the ring.

"Guzman," Josh said.

I watched for a few seconds. "The white guy?" I asked. Josh nodded.

"He's got nothing in his right. Doesn't put anything behind it."

"You think you're telling me something I don't already know, mister?" Josh said without looking at me. "He's got a left, good left, and he's got the heart, but no punch. Guzman ain't no main-eventer."

"The other guy looks pretty good," I said.

"Yeah, you tell me Bobby's problem."

I watched the two of them going at it again. Guzman did have a pretty good left and maybe he could take a punch, but there was no way he could make it through a round with Joe Louis. Ralph Howard had made some poor investments in the boxing world.

"Upstairs, downstairs," I said. "Bobby headhunts and goes for the basket. No change-up."

"Won't go to the heart," Josh said, shaking his head and

pointing to his own heart. "Don't know why. He don't know why. Some fighters are like that. Seen some good fighters, maybe even great fighters. Boy named James Pulley, middle-weight a few years back. Had everything but held back when he went to the head. Didn't want to hurt nobody. Couldn't break him of it."

"Sounds like Howard would have invested a chunk in Pulley if he were still around," I went on as Guzman blocked a left to the head and threw a halfhearted right.

"Howard didn't know fighters," Josh said. "They're like horses. Some of them look great on the outside, like Bobby in there, but something's missing."

"But Lipparini knows the score," I said, watching his face. He turned to look at me, ran his thumb along his gray sideburns.

"Some," he said cautiously.

"Then why did he take a piece of Howard's action?"

"Mister," Josh said softly, "I got me a pretty good living here. People want me to train their fighters, and I do my best, though I don't have a real contender. I'm a good cut man, and I've been in the corner of some boys who've been in there with champions. It's a pretty fair life for an ex-welter who left the ring with no savings and not much in the way of learning. I'd sort of like to enjoy it, not get anybody riled up, and mind my own business."

"I follow," I said.

"Good," Josh said with a grin. "Now I'll answer your damn question. I'd sort of like to do all those things, but I can't live with myself running scared. Mister Lipparini's one of those guys who like to rub up with fighters, ringside, stuff like that. Likes his picture in the papers. He'll rub with the whites and the Negros just so the Negro fighters don't rub too close."

"You don't much care for Mr. Lipparini," I guessed as Guzman threw a good body and head combination. Bobby acted as if he felt nothing.

"Not much," Josh agreed. "Too many like him around the game. Trying to make a dirty dollar. It don't make you a man by buying men. I figure maybe Lipparini buys fighters and sells them 'cause he got something missing. I figure he went in with Mister Howard because Howard looked clean and respectable and Lipparini wanted to dirty him up a little."

"You figure pretty well," I said as Josh threw the towel into the ring. It thudded against Guzman's back.

"That'll do it," Josh called. "Go get something to eat and come back in an hour."

"One final question," I said. "How come they call him Teeth Guzman?"

"On account of he ain't got any," Josh said.

My question answered, I made my way around a guy jumping rope and a kid with pretty good muscles who looked as if he were trying real hard to push down the wall.

Parkman's outer office door was open. I went in. There was no one around. In the daylight I could now see that the walls out here were covered with posters announcing past fight cards. I'd seen some of them, including the Henry Armstrong exhibition last year. I went through the outer office, knocked at the door of the inner one, and went in before Parkman could answer. He was sitting there looking scared.

"Go," he said. His little mustache twitched. He was dressed in another less than elegant but glowing suit. This one was almost white with gold threads.

"I can't. You're a suspect."

"Me?" he pointed at his chest. "Me? A suspect? For what?"

"Murder. Ralph Howard's."

"I . . . He owed me money," Parkman sputtered. "I couldn't murder. Lipparini . . ."

I waited till he lapsed into coherence. It took a while.

"Okay, okay," he said, getting up. "I couldn't kill anybody. I liked Howard. I mean he was a class guy. You don't get a lot of class guys in a business like this."

I pulled up a chair and sat down, saying nothing. My eyes wandered around the room looking at pictures of King Levinsky, Jack Sharkey, and Bob Pastor. Parkman was strong on the heavyweights.

"Who else might have wanted Howard dead?" I asked. "I'll give you some names. You give me a make on any you know."

I pulled out my list from Ralph's notebook, placed it on the desk, flattened it with my palm, and read a name. "Mahan, Jeffrey."

"Means nothing to me," he said. His eyes went to the door. I looked but there was no one there.

"Let's try Dolph Heitner."

"Light heavy," Parkman said, picking up a pencil and putting it down. "You know you broke my lamp last night?"

"I know," I said. "Send me a bill. A light heavy?"

"Yeah," he sighed. "Howard had a piece of him, too. Figured with a Kraut name we could get some good spots on the card. People might come out to see him get plastered."

"And?"

"Heitner joined the Navy." Parkman half-laughed. "By the time the war's over, if he makes it through, he'll be too old to fight and, assuming we win, no one is going to be interested in a third-rater just because he has a Kraut name. Howard could pick 'em all right. And Lipparini was right in there with them. Funny, isn't it? I'm supposed to be the cheap manager who doesn't dress too classy, and these two smart, rich guys with all the connections are buying washed-up fighters I wouldn't take for nothing and paying me to manage them. You know what I'm talking?"

I was telling him I knew when his eyes went to the door again. Again I looked, but this time there was someone there: Mush and Silvio.

"Oh no," Parkman said, looking at the window, realizing he'd never make it, and then collapsing into his chair.

"They're going to . . . I didn't tell this guy a thing, not a thing. Ask him."

"No a thing," I agreed, standing up to face them.

I could see the pattern of blue veins on Mush's shaven head. Some people look good with their heads shaved. Others look like Mush. Silvio stepped forward. I thought about the window, too, but agreed with Parkman. I'd never make it.

Mush closed the door.

"I've got a deal with Lipparini," I reminded them.

"We're canceling it," Mush said, reaching for my collar. I threw a low right, but it bounced off his stomach. I tried for another right as he got a grip of my neck, but he blocked it with his shoulder. I could feel Silvio stepping in to get a shot at me.

"Monty isn't going to like this," I tried.

"You aren't going to be around to tell him," Silvio said behind me.

"Wait," Parkman said and then shut up when Silvio slammed his fist down on the desk. Things certainly did not look good. Mush and Silvio were pros, not just pro killers but pro fighters. They had the weight, the experience, and the years on me, and I was going to get hurt very badly if I was lucky. I had the feeling they had worse in mind for me than split lips and broken bones. If Lipparini sent them, he had decided my nonexistent files weren't enough to keep him from his duty. If Lipparini didn't send them, then they were going against the boss, and they wouldn't want me alive to complain. I made another shot at keeping my skin by trying a very low left, but Mush turned and caught it on his thigh without easing up on my neck. Things were going dark and inky inside my head, and I was afraid I'd soon be seeing my old pal Koko the Clown. This time when I went into the inkwell with him, I probably wouldn't be coming out.

I'm not sure if I heard the door open or just imagined later I did. The grip on my neck loosened enough for me to open my eyes. There was a soldier standing there, a corporal dressed in brown and filling the door. His face was blank and brown and beautiful.

"You'd best let him go," Louis said, tucking his cap into his belt.

Mush didn't let me go. Instead he threw a right into my stomach that made me feel like a kid with the bad part of the flu. I needed what my brother and I used to call a throw-up bucket. I cracked against the desk and tried to grab something to keep from falling, but there was nothing to grab. I slipped to the floor.

"You'd best get out," Louis said to Mush and Silvio, but they were committed. It was too late. Silvio's hand went under his jacket and I lurched forward on my knees, hitting him low with my shoulder. He pulled his hand out of his jacket and used his hands to keep from going over the chair. That was all I had in me. I was on my back, looking up, when Mush threw the first punch at Louis.

The champ's left shot out to block the punch, and he followed with a right and left to Mush's stomach. Silvio, on the blind side, picked up the chair in one hand and pulled it back to fling it at Louis. The champ stepped forward under the chair and threw a right and left combination to the midsection. Silvio went down hard. Mush was up, his arms out, trying to grab Louis around the waist, but Louis stepped back against the wall, crouched, and threw a pair of rat-tat lefts at his chest. Both punches were jabs. Mush went down for the count.

"See," Parkman shouted behind the desk. "Body punches. All body punches."

"Didn't want to break my hands," Louis explained, helping me up. "These are the two I saw there on the beach."

"It's getting curious," I said, unable to stand up.

"Take small breaths," Louis advised. "Real small, like a dog."

I panted. It helped.

"What are you doing here?" I asked when I could. "Not that I'm complaining."

"Came looking for Mr. Parkman," Louis explained. "Settle up for the workout and to see Josh. I want him to work my corner after the war, with Chappie and Roxie gone."

"I'll drink to that," I said, propping myself on the desk and looking around with eyes that felt as if they might pop out of the sockets. Mush and Silvio were down, but only Mush was out. Silvio was moaning low.

"Call the cops," I told Parkman. "Champ, you'd better do some roadwork. I'll try to keep you clean on this, but you might have to identify our two sparring partners."

"If you say so," Louis said. "Sure you can handle them, now?"

I reached down and took the gun out from under Silvio's jacket. He moaned some more and tried to find his stomach with his right hand, but it eluded him.

Behind us, Parkman was talking into the phone.

I walked with Louis out of the outer office and into the gym.

"I got to go back to New York," he said. "Might have to go tomorrow unless I get mixed up with this. Truth is I want to get back to my wife. We tried for a baby last year. Marva had a miscarriage."

The action in the gym had almost come to a stop. People were looking at Louis instead of their bags and sparring partners.

"It's going to be hard to deny you were here," I said, looking around. Louis looked, too.

"Do what you can," he said, taking my hand. "You can find me at the Braxton Hotel at least through tomorrow."

I turned back into the alcove near Al Parkman's office after I watched Corporal Louis pat China Rogers on the back and disappear down the steps. The door to the outer office was locked, which I didn't like. I hadn't even closed the door. I liked even less the six shots that came from behind it. I threw my elbow into the rectangle with Parkman's name on it, let the glass clear, and reached in to open the door. I could hear steps behind me from the gym, running to see what was going on.

Glass crunched under my feet, and I felt pain in my stomach from the blow Mush had thrown, but I knew I'd feel worse if Parkman was dead.

The inner door was locked, too, and it was harder to get through. I threw my shoulder against it and pleaded with my stomach not to turn against me just yet. The door didn't open. I stepped back and kicked it three or four times, and it popped open.

Silvio and Mush were still in place on the floor, only the count was final now. There were spots of red, three on Silvio's face, little holes. Dripping red. He looked surprised. Mush was on his stomach. At least one bullet had gone into his back.

And Parkman? Parkman was gone.

6

"**O**kay, little brother," Phil said, slamming the top drawer of his desk two hours later. "Where do we start?"

The pile of reports, files, and odd scraps of paper in front of Phil was about four inches high. He patted it, rubbed his meaty right hand on the surface of his desk, and looked at me. Phil's office was big and empty. It echoed. He had spent almost a decade in the small lieutenant's cubbyhole in the squadroom down the hall. In the month he had been in this new office, he had made no effort to adjust to it, fit into it. Maybe he felt he wouldn't be there long, that he would be back in his cubbyhole when the war ended and younger vets came home. His temper had kept him in that cubbyhole longer than he should have been there, a temper that crackled at nearby criminals, whose rights ended at Phil's knuckles.

The wooden floor of Phil's office was stained with years of grime. The desk was the battered one his predecessor Capt. Fred Molin had left behind. The window was uncovered, and there were no pictures on the brown walls. A file cabinet did stand in one corner and Steve Seidman leaned against it listening.

After I found the bodies of Mush and Silvio, I had made my way through the pack of boxers trying to see what was happening, and had gone through the gym and down the steps. Gunther was gone. I was just heading back to Reed's when the squad car came flying down Figueroa, full siren. Parkman had called them during the fight. They would find more than a couple of bloody noses.

Now I sat looking at Phil, who reached up to loosen his collar, which was already unbuttoned. I didn't know where to start.

"No answer?" he said. "Then I'll pick a place." He pulled off the top report.

"Ferdinand 'Mush' Margolis, thirty-two, automobile salesman," he read and then looked up. "Mush did very well as a car salesman last year in spite of the fact that there were no cars to sell. Very enterprising young man except when he got into a little trouble here and there. Look here. We even have an arrest for murder. Never went to trial. One scar on the face, cause unknown."

He put the report on the side and took up the next one.

"Silvio Defatto, twenty-nine, also a car salesman. Like Margolis, he seems to have had a reasonably successful boxing career back East. Beyond that his life is sadly lacking in detail."

Phil put this report away, too, and looked at me.

"Your friend Parkman is not a pro at shooting people," he said. "Point blank in a small room, and he hit them all over the place. It took him everything he had in the gun to kill them."

"He might have been scared," I suggested.

"They were lying on the goddamn floor for chrissake," he shouted. "And where the hell is Parkman? He's not back at his house. The way he was dressed we should be able to spot him two blocks away in the dark. Next item." This report was a bit thicker than the first two.

"Joseph Louis Barrow. Born May 13, 1914, Lafayette, Alabama. Current weight two hundred pounds. Height six feet, one and a half inches. Managed by John Roxborough, now in prison, and trained by the late Jack Blackburn, who was once convicted of murder. Joseph Louis Barrow of Detroit, who, according to you, happens to have been jogging on the beach when a man was beaten to death and happens to have run into the same two men in a gym a few hours ago just before they were murdered. You did a great job of keeping him out of trouble, Tobias."

"There—" I began.

"I entered the name Joseph Barrow of Detroit on the report," Seidman said from the corner. "We sent Cawelti and Burns to talk to him."

"Phil—" I began, but he cut me off again, holding up his left hand.

"There's more," he said, opening the folder in front of him. "Your corpse on the beach, identified by Anne, who didn't have much to identify. According to the medical examiner, he didn't die on the beach. Not enough blood in the sand. He was dead a couple of hours when you got there. If Louis saw Defatto and Margolis with the body, they were dumping him, bringing him home."

"So Louis is off the hook?" I said.

"If," Seidman said behind us, "he can get someone to say he was with her two hours before the discovery of the body."

"I told you the problem there," I said. "He was with a woman, a white—"

Phil got up from behind the desk, took the folder on Ralph Howard, and threw it at me. "I don't give a shit who he was with," he shouted. "I want a name."

"No fuss, no muss, no publicity," Seidman said. "We just talk to her. She says he was with her, we just prepare a single-sheet report and put it in the investigation file. Discoverer of the body, Joseph Barrow of Detroit, reported seeing two men leaving the location where body was discovered. Barrow's presence at the time of the actual murder was established by a reliable citizen, and we fill in the name. That's it."

I reached for the phone on Phil's desk. He sat back while I got the Braxton and Joe Louis's room. I told him two cops were on the way to talk to him, told him he wouldn't wind up in the newspapers, and asked for the name of the woman in Santa Monica who would give him the alibi. It took a promise I wasn't sure I could deliver to get the name and address, but I got them. I hung up smiling. The name he had given me was more than familiar. I gave Phil the name.

"Meara's waiting outside," Phil said. "He figures the Howard killing and this afternoon's shooting gallery are tied together, and he's damn right. He wants to talk to you again. He wants reports. He wants results. Everybody wants."

"And you're going to give him . . ." I said.

"Shit," said Phil, shouting. "Shit, shit, shit."

"Phil," Seidman said gently, stepping from the corner. "Take it easy. You've got it all under control."

Phil glared at me, his face a fleshy pink. His right hand had crushed a sheet of paper and he was squeezing it as if it were Meara's neck. Or mine. He shrugged, nodded in agreement, threw the crumpled paper on his desk, and sat again, opening the final and thickest folder.

"Lipparini," he read, "Monty. Owner of M. L. Auto Sales. Wife Chloe, three kids. Investments all over the valley. Just opened the M. L. Coffee Company in Encino. Respectable businessman, right? Three or four arrests when he was younger. No convictions. Brought in for questioning more times than I can count. But an honest citizen, right?"

"Right," I agreed. I knew that look in Phil's eyes, that wild look.

"Wrong," he shouted, rubbing his hand across the steely bristles on his head. "Wrong. The maggot is a killer. He killed at least two people in Jersey before he came here. It's in the report, but there was no evidence, no witnesses. He killed a woman in Los Angeles six years ago. Only witness disappeared. Since then he's had other people do his killing."

"Like Mush and Silvio," I suggested.

"Mush and Silvio," he agreed. "And Lipparini has parties with movie stars and gets his picture in the papers. And Steve can't get enough money together to buy a house, and I can't pay off my kid's hospital bills."

Phil's son, my nephew Dave, had been hit by a car a few years back. The doctor's bills had wiped out Phil's savings. He didn't know it, but I had kicked in a few bucks to his wife Ruth from time to time when I had a few, which, I realized, I now had.

"You think Lipparini had Howard killed?" he asked.

"I don't know, Phil," I said. "Maybe. Why don't you ask him?"

"Meara's asking him now, in my old office," he said. "Two of his salesmen get killed, you think the man might have an idea or two. You think Meara's going to get hamster shit out of Lipparini?"

"No," I said.

"No," Phil agreed. "So we keep looking for Parkman, and Lipparini goes off to some country club dance. We look for Parkman and hope we get to him before Lipparini, who might not like flashy little fight promoters punctuating his hired help. Things like that happen enough, and you might lose some credibility in the business."

"You want me to go with Meara?" I said.

Phil didn't answer. His elbows were on the desk and his head in his hands.

"You want Toby to go with Meara?" Seidman repeated.

"Get out," Phil said without looking up. "You think this is the only case we're working on? I've still got the Citizens to Prevent Crime coming in this afternoon. A group of businessmen who think the Mexicans in the zoot suits are going to organize and come after them with key chains and machetes. And we've got the asshole in MacArthur Park who keeps showing his dong to old ladies. And I still haven't finished the damn duty roster. Get out."

"Phil, I . . ." I began. Usually at this point I'd come up with a few words to provoke him into fury, but I didn't have the heart.

"Just take off, Toby," Seidman said. "I've got an appointment with Minck at ten in the morning. Maybe I'll see you then."

Phil looked up, started to put the reports in a neat pile, and said gruffly, "Go on. I'll be all right. Maybe I'll get Meara to lose his temper so I can squeeze his fat neck till his red little eyes pop."

The idea seemed to cheer Phil a bit, so I went out into the hall and closed the door behind me. I might be able to catch Lipparini if I hurried. So I hurried, pushed through the squadroom door, and looked over the room filled with cops, creeps, and bewildered honest citizens. No one seemed to have made even a halfhearted attempt to clean the floor since I'd last been here. The massive Sergeant Veldu was sitting against his desk eating a burger and listening to a thin, scraggly woman with a high voice who leaned forward toward him and gestured with both hands.

"He had on a coat," she said. "I said to myself, 'Who needs a coat in this weather?' That's what I asked myself. Then I found out. Open comes the coat and there's nothing under."

"What'd he look like?" Veldu said through a mouthful.

"I dunno," the woman screamed. "All I could see was his thing."

"What'd that look like?" Veldu asked.

"A hairy popsicle," she said and Veldu choked, gasped, and coughed, sending a spray of burger, lettuce, and bun in the general direction of a wild-haired kid handcuffed to a nearby chair.

"What're you laughing at?" the woman said. "It's not funny."

Veldu kept laughing as the handcuffed kid whimpered, "Hey, watch what you're chewing there, huh?"

I passed some faces I knew, a few guys in uniform, a few not, and made my way to Phil's old office. I knocked and went in. Meara was leaning against the desk. The light was off.

"Where's Lipparini?" I asked.

"Gone," he said. "Bastard had his lawyer with him. Gives me a statement, says those guys just worked for him, and the lawyer says that's it. I wanted to rip his dago guts out."

"That would have wrapped up the case nicely," I said.

Meara pushed himself from the desk, straightened his jacket, and looked at me. He tried for a nasty smile, but his heart wasn't in it. He was just going through the motions.

"This is my case," he said, pointing to himself so I would know who he was talking about. "I don't think those two wops Parkman plugged killed Howard."

"One of those wops was a Jew," I corrected him.

"All the same," he said with a sweep of his hand to clear the matter up. He was deep in his own thoughts. "Lipparini knows something. I could feel it right in my fingers. If I could have worked him just ten minutes. Just ten minutes. Lord, is that too much to ask? I go to church."

If it hadn't been clear before, it was now. Meara had a tankful. He took a not-too-steady step toward me.

"I am one hell of a good cop," he said.

"One hell of a good cop," I repeated.

"And my kid is one hell of a good soldier," he said defiantly.

"A good soldier," I agreed.

I left him standing in the dark office and went back into the squadroom. The damn station was beginning to depress me, but I should have known better than to have expected the bluebird of happiness in the Wilshire Station. If said avian had accidentally flown in, the cops would have blown its head off and one of the grifters would have had its feathers out in less than the time it takes to say, "Duz does everything." I didn't look at Veldu or the complaining woman or the handcuffed kid. I made it to the door and ran down the stairs.

I found a phone in the grocery store around the corner

and called the M. L. Auto Sales office. The blonde in green answered.

"Mr. Lipparini," I said. "This is Toby Peters."

She put the phone down for a few seconds and then came back with, "He is not here and does not want to talk to you."

"Tell him—" I started, and she hung up.

While I considered what to do next, I picked up some essentials in the grocery, a carton of milk for twelve cents, some donuts for another twelve, and three eleven-ounce packages of Sunnyfield Corn Flakes for twenty cents. I paid the old lady behind the counter and went back to the phone. Almost half a buck for a small sack of groceries.

When the blonde answered this time, I did my imitation of Lionel Stander and said, "It's Joe. I gotta talk to Mr. Lipparini."

"Joe?" she said. "Joe Salter?"

"Yeah, yeah," I growled. "Put him on."

"He already left for the party," she said. "I mean he's going home first and then—"

"Where's the party?" I growled impatiently.

"At Marty's Lounge," she said.

"On Beverly?"

"Yes, but—" she began. I didn't hear the rest. This time I hung up on her.

I got into my car, which the police had parked in a no-parking zone in front of the station. It was a game they enjoyed playing. I took the ticket from the windshield, stuffed it into my pocket, opened the door, and put my groceries down.

It was late afternoon when I got back to Mrs. Plaut's. The landlady was nowhere in sight. She was probably making her daily rounds of the neighbors to strong-arm them into turning over sugar-ration coupons.

Two little girls who lived next door had set up a *Kool-Aid 1¢* sign. I shifted my package and pulled out a penny. The older girl, about five, took the penny and poured red liquid from a glass pitcher into a coffee cup. The coffee cup didn't look clean. I tasted the drink. It contained no sugar.

"Good," I said, belting down the remainder.

"Henry helped us make it," the smaller girl said. Her face was round, outlined by straight brown hair.

"Henry makes good Kool-Aid," I said with a smile.

"Henry is our dog," the other girl said.

I put down the cup and hurried up the steps and into the house. Before I parked my groceries, I knocked on Gunther's door.

"Come in, Toby," he said and in I went.

He was seated at his desk on his child's chair. The desk was low, a normal model with the legs cut off. The walls of the room were lined from floor to ceiling with books, except for the alcove near the window where Gunther's refrigerator and dining table stood. His window was covered with a white curtain that let the light in. In one corner of the room was Gunther's small bed, neatly made, a normal sofa, which matched the one in my room, and a reading lamp.

"Toby," he said, turning to me with his hands out, "I'm sorry. I was unable to pursue them to their ultimate destination."

"Pursue who, Gunther?"

"Mr. Al Parkman and the man he came out with, out from the gymnasium." He pronounced it "gym-nah-zi-um."

"Take it slow and tell me what happened."

"I almost missed them initially," he said. "They emerged from the alley next to the theater. Mr. Al Parkman's clothing is such that I noticed him. He does not dress tastefully."

"The other man?" I asked patiently.

"Difficult to describe with great accuracy," Gunther said, pondering the question. "No higher than you, perhaps even near the same weight. He wore the blue wool hat of a merchant sailor. I did not clearly see his face and I did not see his hair. He wore a blue pea coat. Of his age I can say only that he was not a very young man and not a very old man."

"Could 'he' have been a 'she'?"

"It is of course possible," Gunther said, putting his fingertips together, "but I do not think so. They were too far away for me to conjecture beyond that which I have so far done. They entered a small car and drove. I followed. They drove to the Pasadena Freeway. There was much traffic, and I lost them just after the Orange Grove Avenue. I am sorry."

The freeway had opened two years earlier with bands, tape, and a dedication by Mayor Fletcher Brown, who said the freeway would save lives. The lanes were narrow, the curves sharp, there were no shoulders and not enough merging space on the ramps. It was easy to lose your life, let alone someone you were following, on the Pasadena Freeway.

"Nothing to be sorry about, Gunther," I said.

"I returned to Al Parkman's house for an hour," said Gunther. "He did not come, but the police arrived, remained for some time, and then departed. So I came here. I will be happy to resume my vigil at his home should you—"

"No need," I said, shifting my package. "I've got a lead or two. I'm working on one tonight."

Gunther wished me well and I went into the hall, found a nickel, and called Anne to bring her up to date. I told her what I was going to do. She told me not to. I said I would, and she told me to get in touch when I found out anything.

I dined on corn flakes, coffee, and a small can of salmon well mixed with mayo. My suit was showing wear, but I had no time to shop. I brushed myself off and drove downtown to the Farraday Building. I didn't bother to go to No-Neck Arnie's. I had only one thing to do in the office. I parked on the street and hurried into the building and up the stairs. Shelly was changing into his civilian clothes when I entered the office. Little by little the world of Sheldon-crud was reclaiming the room, a crumpled smock on a chair, a pile of less than clean instruments on a tray, the sink more full than it had been a few hours earlier.

"Calls?" I asked.

"No calls," he said.

I took the five quick steps to my office before he could say more. Inside I went to my desk, found the Blake poems in the drawer, pulled out two one-hundred-dollar bills and an envelope to put them in. The envelope said WARNER BROTHERS STUDIO in the corner. I crossed it out. I folded the bills into a sheet of paper, stuffed it all into the envelope, and licked it closed and put it in my pocket.

When I got back to the outer office, Shelly was still there, standing with his arms at his side. He looked like a pathetic meatball.

"What's the problem, Shel?" I asked before I could stop myself.

"Mildred," he said. "She's in Sacramento visiting her mother."

"That's nice, Shel," I said, going for the door.

"I've got nothing to do tonight," he said. "No one to eat with. You know how that is."

"Enjoy it, Shel. It doesn't happen often. You deserve it." My hand was on the doorknob, and I almost made it.

"How about you and I having dinner together?" he said as if he had just thought of it. "On me. I mean if we don't go anywhere too . . ."

"Gotta work, Shel," I said. "There's a party I have to crash and—"

"A party," he said, moving toward me and adjusting his glasses. "I haven't crashed a party since I was in college. Cal Fleischer and I crashed the Beta Phi pledge party. That's how I met Mildred."

"I thought you met Mildred after you graduated, at a dental convention," I said. "You hired her as your dental assistant."

"That's right," he said, snapping his fingers. "That was Jenny something I met at the Phi Beta Party."

"Beta Phi," I corrected. "You won't like this party, Shel. Believe me."

"Okay," he said, moving to his dental chair. "Okay, I know when I'm not wanted. I'll just get a sandwich and sit here. Maybe I'll listen to the radio or something. You just go on ahead and crash your party."

Normally, Shelly did not know when he wasn't wanted even when it was made as clear as I was making it.

"Come on, Shel," I said. "But don't blame me if it's not what you expect."

"Hah," Shelly cackled, jumping up. "I knew I could count on you, Toby. We'll have fun. You'll see. And what Mildred doesn't know . . ."

"Right," I said. "Let's go."

He followed me out of the door through the small waiting room and into the hallway of the fourth floor of the Farraday. Someone was chanting in a foreign language down the hall.

"Whose party are we crashing?" Shelly said eagerly.

"Fella named Lipparini," I told him. The name didn't seem to mean anything to him.

We made one stop. It was far out of the way, but I had to make it. I drove up Laurel Canyon to the Valley and made my way to Bluebelle Street in North Hollywood. I told Shelly he could come in, but he preferred to stay in the car and rest for the big night ahead, which was fine with me. The screen door was open and I called, "Anyone here?"

"Toby?" came Ruth's voice, followed by Ruth carrying Lucy, who was now old enough to walk but not very interested in that means of transportation. Ruth was skinny, tired, with tinted blond hair that wouldn't stay up, and a gentle smile. Lucy looked at me with round brown eyes that showed recognition.

"Uncle Toby," she said to her mother and scrambled to be let down.

"Where are the boys?" I said.

"In back," my sister-in-law said. "I'll get them. Toby, what happened to your face?"

Lucy had scrambled to me and I picked her up, checking her hands to be sure they weren't concealing weapons. Lucy had a pet lock she liked to suck on and use to tap out a tune on an unsuspecting victim. She had her father's blood in her, that girl did. She also had the same favorite victim: me.

"A little scrape with the law," I said, stopping myself from touching my cheek.

"Phil?" she asked softly.

"No," I said. "Phil and I are getting along like brothers."

"Cain and Abel," she supplied.

"Daddy shoots," Lucy informed me, looking into my ear.

"Sometimes," I told her, and then to Ruth, "How is he?"

"He" was my nephew Dave, who had recovered well from the collision with the truck. Dave was nine, and if he kept challenging trucks he would fulfill his destiny as my logical heir.

"He's fine," Ruth said, playing with the collar of her gray dress. "You'll see."

"The bills?" I went on.

"The bills." She shrugged. "You want a cup of coffee?"

"No, I've got to go to a party," I said. "Phil's new job . . ."

"Oh, he got a raise," she said, "a nice raise, but we still owe . . . a lot."

I shifted Lucy into my other arm and she decided it would be interesting if our heads collided. She caught me just below the nose, which hurt her more than it did me. While she screamed, I pulled the envelope with the money out of my pocket. Ruth reached over to take the yowling kid, but I held onto Lucy and handed her the envelope instead.

"Toby I . . ." she said, looking down at the envelope with tears starting.

"Sure you can," I said. "I hit the jackpot. Let me feel like big time once in a while. You think I have something better to do with my money? I'd blow it all on food, clothes, rent, luxury items."

Ruth laughed and found a pocket to put the envelope in. "Thanks," she said, kissing my cheek, the good one. Lucy leaned into my ear and used it for a microphone. I went deaf from her scream and lifted her over me and let her tummy rub against my head. The screams turned to laughter. I'd missed my true calling, kindergarten teacher.

"Don't tell—" I began, but Ruth stopped me.

"I couldn't tell Phil," she said. "Not now, maybe someday."

Lucy was laughing above me now and drooling on my back. I was having a good time.

"It's not worth someday," I said. "Hasn't been that much."

Before this got any more sentimental, Nate and Dave broke into the room. Nate was twelve and practical.

"Uncle Toby, who did you kill yesterday?" Dave shouted. It was his favorite question. He pushed his dark hair from his forehead and waited for my answer.

"Yesterday?" I said, putting Lucy down on the floor to scurry in search of her lock or some other weapon. "What about today? I put a hole through the head of a killer named Weasel Fultch and maybe three or four others. It's hard to keep track."

Nate shook his head tolerantly. He was too old for such tales, but there was enough about me that kept him off balance and left open the possibility that some of my tales of mayhem might be true.

"That's how I got this bruise," I said, pointing to my cheek. "The Weasel threw a boomerang at me. I ducked just in time and took a shot at him before the boomerang came back on its second pass."

Ruth was leaning against the wall, her skinny arms folded, shaking her head.

"A boomerang?" Dave said, moving close to examine my cheek, which I turned to him so he could have a good look.

"Razor sharp," I said. "I won't have to shave that side of my face for a month. What were you guys playing?"

"Mr. Fate," Dave said. "You want to come out in the yard and play with us?"

"Can't," I said as Lucy came back into the room with a big smile and toddled toward me with her lock in hand. "I've got to get to this party a big gangster is throwing and try to talk him out of killing me."

"Uncle Toby," Nate sighed, shaking his head just like his mother. I danced out of the path of Lucy, and she plunged gleefully into the sofa. This was her favorite game.

"How do you play Mr. Fate?" I said, keeping an eye on Lucy, who was organizing herself for another attack.

"You point your finger at someone like this," Dave said, pointing his finger at me, "and say 'Laxo.' Then the person you're pointing at gets diarrhea. It's a super power."

"Very effective." I grinned.

Lucy came at me and Nate yelled, "Lulu, no."

She missed me and tumbled into her brother's arms. Nate took the lock from her hand, and Lucy started to cry again, reaching for her toy.

"Can you take us out, Uncle Tobe?" Dave asked.

"Not today," I said, aiming for the door and giving Ruth a wave. "I'm late for that party. Besides, I've got a case. I'm working for Joe Louis."

"Joe Louis?" Nate said, still holding the lock from his sister. "He was in the comics."

"And the ring," I said. "He's the heavyweight champ of the world."

"I know that," said Nate as Lucy advanced on him, mouth open, to sink her few teeth into his leg.

"Are you going to fight him?" Dave asked, ignoring the by-play of his sister and brother.

"Naw," I said. "I'm giving him a few tips, but it wouldn't look good for him to get into the ring with me. Think of the embarrassment if I hurt him."

"I see," Dave said seriously.

"I'll take you to a movie Saturday if your mom says okay. *Elephant Boy* with Sabu," I said as I pushed open the screen door.

"Great," Nate said.

"Great," Dave repeated.

"You don't have to copy everything," Nate said, making a face at his brother.

Dave did a Mr. Fate and pointed his lethal Ex-Lax finger at his brother, who feigned a sudden attack of the lower abdomen.

"Thanks, Toby," Ruth called. I waved and went out to join Shelly for our night on the town.

7

The sun was just going down when we pulled up half a block away from Marty's Lounge on Beverly in Beverly Hills.

"That's it," I told Shelly, who strained to see through his glasses and the windshield.

"Classy," he said appreciatively.

"Classy," I agreed and got out of the car.

Marty's Lounge was a two-story brick place with only a small sign at the entrance to indicate its name. MARTY was tastefully etched in white on an amber window. Next to it was a white outlined caricature of a man with a massive nose, probably Marty.

We entered and took a few seconds to adjust to the near darkness.

"Can I help you, sir?" came a deep voice. I made out a man in a tux a few feet in front of me. He looked a little like William Powell.

"A table," I said.

"Name?" he shot back.

"Peter," I said.

He checked the list on the table and shook his head. "I'm sorry," he purred, "but you have no reservation. Perhaps another night?"

"I'm with the Lipparini party," I said.

"I'm sorry," he said again, "but Mr. Lipparini left the names of all the guests, and your name is not on the list."

"Look . . ." I began.

The man in the tux turned to the table and pressed a button.

"Another night," I said, moving toward the door.

"Another night," the man said with a pleasant smile.

"That's it?" Shelly said on the street. "That's how you crash a party?"

"I'm not finished," I said, walking toward the corner.

"A party crasher, you are not," Shelly said, waddling along at my side.

"Then go home," I growled. "Get a cab and go home. Coming with me was your idea."

"You need my help here." He grinned as we hit the corner. "I'll show you how to crash a party."

Shelly scooted ahead of me around the corner, and I hurried to keep up with him. At the back of the building he made another turn, and I followed. We were in an alleyway, but a nice clean alleyway, everything in shiny cans with lids. A person could live in an alley like this.

"There," Shelly shouted triumphantly, pointing at a rear entrance. "Let's go."

He opened the door and went in with me behind, and we almost ran into two gentlemen in tuxedoes. One of the two was big, the other small. Both looked tough and both had clear bulges under their coats where their hearts should have been but where hardware resided instead.

"Where you going?" the smaller one said.

"Going?" asked Shelly.

"To the party," I said.

The two looked us up and down.

"We're late," Shelly went on.

"You're the extra waiters?" the smaller one asked.

"Who else?" Shelly asked.

"I thought they couldn't get extra waiters?" the big hood asked in return.

"We were at another party, big dinner for George Raft," I said. "Overstaffed."

"George Raft is at this party," the big one said suspiciously.

"That's why we were sent here," Shelly explained.

This seemed to both satisfy and confuse the two, who stepped back.

"Uniforms are in the room over there," the big one said. "Get a move on. They already started."

I pushed through the door with Shelly at my side, and we found ourselves alone in a small locker room.

"Damn, this is fun," Shelly beamed, puffing out his cheeks. "George Raft is here."

"I'm thrilled and delighted," I said, looking for another way out of the room. There was none. The only way out was past the two armed penguins. We found a rack of uniforms in the corner and put two of them on, Shelly with glee, me with foreboding.

"Wait till I tell Mildred about this," Sheldon said, putting on a pair of black pants with a red stripe. "On second thought, maybe I'd better not."

"Suit yourself, Shel," I said.

"I won't forget you for this, Toby," he said, picking out the fattest maroon jacket on the rack. I grunted, found a shirt and maroon bow tie, and got dressed. The jacket I finally selected fit fine across the shoulders, though the sleeves were a little short. We were surveying ourselves in the mirror when the door to the room opened and the smaller thug yelled, "Shake your asses."

We moved into the hallway with him holding the door open for us. "That way, to the left," he said, and we moved.

When we pushed through the hinged double door, we found ourselves in a lunatic asylum of a kitchen. Two chefs in white were facing each other and shouting. One had a walrus mustache and wore a chef's cap that bounced on his head.

The other chef was thin. His hat kept threatening to cover his eyes. Around them, waiters bustled, picking up trays, barely missing each other.

"I'll take this knife," the one with the walrus mustache shouted, holding up a knife that looked like the sword Errol Flynn carried in *The Sea Hawk,* "I'll take this knife and slice you into shashlik before I let you garnish the potatoes."

"Slice," said the thinner chef defiantly, his hands on his hips. "Slice. You don't know how to season a hot dog, you Austrian schnitzel."

The walrus chef raised the knife over his head while Shelly and I watched. The waiters scurried around the chefs, paying no attention, though one mumbled, "Scuse me," as he brushed past.

Then the thin chef spotted us. "So, what are you waiting?" he shouted while the walrus chef stood patiently holding the knife in the air. "You've got tables seven and twelve. We're on the soup."

"Seven and twelve," I repeated.

"Soup," said Shelly.

We got into the stream of waiters, and each of us picked up a tray covered with bowls of soup. I tried to hold the tray up like the other waiters, balancing it on one hand and holding it with the other over my shoulder. The bowls slid but didn't spill.

"What are you?" bellowed the walrus chef.

"New at this," I apologized.

Shelly had picked up his tray and was bounding happily toward the door through which the other maroon-clad waiters were hurrying.

The walrus chef handed his sword to the thin chef, who took it. Then the walrus chef showed me how to hold the tray. "Like this, like this. What were you before you became a waiter?"

"An exterminator," I said.

"There is no humor in that," he said seriously. "Move."

He took the knife back from the thin chef as I barely missed an incoming waiter. Juggling soup bowls, I went through the big double doors and then through a brown velvet drapery that had been opened enough for us waiters to pass through. I found myself in a huge room where the sounds of people laughing played over and under a five-piece band in the corner that was belting out "Silver Dollar."

There were tables all over the place and on a slightly raised platform against the far wall, a long table. In the middle of the long table sat Lipparini. His head was cocked to the side. He was listening seriously to an old man who whispered to him. On the other side of Lipparini sat a woman in a blue gown, her hair dark, piled high, and lacquered on her head.

I found my table by the big number twelve planted in the center of it next to a bowl of flowers. A small table between two tables let me put the tray down. Two tables down at number seven, Shelly was just finishing doling out his bowls.

I couldn't remember which side to serve the soup from. There was no time to worry about it. I just handed it out, and no one at the table seemed to mind except one too-thin and almost pretty, heavily made-up woman, who gave me a dirty look. I smiled apologetically and went for more soup.

"You know who I just served soup to?" Shelly whispered loudly over the band, which had gone into a rendition of "Amapola." "I just served soup to Wallace Beery. Or maybe it was Noah Beery. Whoever he is, he has some really fine dentures."

"Great," I said, looking around to see how I could get to Lipparini. The prospects weakened when I saw a tuxedo-clad Moe, the last of the Stooges, step directly behind Lipparini.

"You think it would be out of place to slip Mr. Beery one of my cards?" Shelly said. "Or you think it might be a little too . . ."

"A little too," I said.

"Maybe I could stick cards on the plates when we serve

dessert," Shel said. Sweat stains were beginning to appear on his fluffy shirt.

We took our empty trays back into the kitchen and someone who might have been a headwaiter, because his jacket was black instead of maroon, told us to stop fooling around.

We each picked up another tray of soup just as a sweating kid finished filling the bowls. The two chefs were no longer discussing murder. They were huddled over a massive steel pot, looking into it for answers to some deep culinary question.

Shelly waddled happily ahead of me back into the ballroom, and I managed to follow without dumping the soup while I watched Lipparini. After I'd served four of the eight people at my table, I glanced up and saw Lipparini put his napkin next to his plate and get up. He was either going to make a speech or head for the toilet.

"Waiter," someone said below me.

"Shh," I answered without looking down.

"Who the hell are you shushing?" the voice said.

Lipparini excused his way down the long table, and Moe did not follow him. It was time to move.

"I said, who the hell are you shushing?" the voice repeated.

"Sorry," I said. "My wife's having a baby. Serve yourselves."

I grabbed Shelly, who had just finished serving, and shouted, "Let's go," over the tune of "Hindustan."

"Where are we going?" he said. "We just started. Hey look. George Raft is out there dancing. George Raft. Can you imagine?"

I tugged Shelly behind me through the maze of tables and along the edge of the dance floor. We got close enough to George Raft to hear him laugh.

"Do you see those teeth?" Shelly said.

"Beautiful," I said and dragged him through the door Lipparini had just made it through. We were in a tastefully decorated lobby. The carpeting was thick and dark, the walls dark and papered with paintings of race horses and yachts. Real class. A woman, a beauty with long yellow hair down her slender bare back, was sitting in one of the Louis-the-somethingth chairs, dividing her attention between two youngish men in tuxes.

"That's Veronica Lake," Shelly said.

"No it isn't," I said, looking around for Lipparini. I didn't see him but I did find the "Gentlemen's Room" in the corner. He might have gone out in the lobby to make a phone call, but this was a good place to start.

"I tell you that was Veronica Lake," he insisted.

"Right, how were her teeth?"

"Teeth?" he asked with a lewd laugh. "Who was looking at teeth?"

The men's room was elegant, inlaid tile sinks, dispensers for soap, and luckily, no attendant. One of the toilet stalls was closed.

"What are we—" Shelly began, and I clamped a hand over his mouth and put my finger to my lips to keep him quiet.

We waited for about a minute, heard the flush, and watched as the trousers came up and the door opened. Lipparini stepped out.

At first Lipparini saw only two waiters. He walked past us and washed his hands. Then, while he was combing his hair, he looked in the mirror and recognized me.

"What is this?" he said, turning to face us. He looked scared. "You try killing me here and you won't make it to the front door."

"Killing?" Shelly said at my side. "Who's talking killing?"

"Shut up, Shel," I said, and then to Lipparini, "I'm not here to kill you. I'm here to tell you Louis and I had nothing to do with gunning Mush and Silvio."

"Mush and . . . Parkman killed them," he said. "And I

plan to find him and take care of his ticket before the cops turn him up. You know where he is?"

"First, did you send Mush and Silvio to get me?" I asked. "They were at Parkman's to kill me."

Lipparini looked at me as if I were crazy.

"Kill you?" whimpered Shelly. "I thought we were just crashing a party."

"I didn't send them for you," Lipparini said. "I told them to stay away from you. Why would they go after you when they knew what would happen, what I would do?" Lipparini's confidence was coming back. He didn't look frightened anymore, just curious.

"Suppose they took Ralph Howard out on an independent contract," I tried. "A little job on the side. There's no rule against that, is there?"

"Not if they tell me and I get a piece of the pie if there's enough to make it interesting," he said, sitting on the edge of the sink and folding his arms.

"Okay, so let's suppose they made a mistake," I went on. "They took the job, got rid of Howard, and then you told them to lay off of me. But I'm still pushing, and someone figures I might come up with a name, someone who maybe gave Mush and Silvio the Howard contract. So they decide to put me away."

Shelly was sagging somewhere behind me, his visions of a frat night out dissolving with each word. He whimpered softly.

"Keep talking," Lipparini said.

"They come after me, but Louis steps in and keeps me from taking a permanent dive. The guy who hired Mush and Silvio now knows that they can peg him. So, he gets rid of them."

"Parkman," Lipparini said. "Right. I'll find him."

"What if it isn't Parkman, or not Parkman alone," I tried.

"Who?" he asked.

"I'm working on it," I said. "Give me time. Leave Joe Louis alone. Leave me alone. I'll get back to you in, let's make it two days."

The door came open and Moe stepped in while Lipparini was thinking. He had a gun in his hand and it was aimed at Shelly's chest.

"No, no," sobbed Shelly behind me. "Not in a waiter's suit."

"Hold it," cried Lipparini.

If Moe was the one who had given the contract to Mush and Silvio, his best move would be to gun us all down. It might be a little messy, but better than some of the possible alternatives. He stopped.

"Put it away," Lipparini said. "Mr. Peters is going to do some work for us. Mr. Peters is going to find out who killed Mush and Silvio."

"Parkman . . ." Moe began as he reluctantly put the gun away.

Something felt cold, wet, and clammy on my arm, and I realized Shelly was clinging to me.

"Maybe not," Lipparini said. "Mr. Peters is going to find out in the next two days. You did say two days, didn't you, Peters?" Lipparini was back in charge and showing lots of teeth, which I thought might interest Shelly if he could stop crying long enough to look.

"Two days," I agreed.

"Friday morning you come up with some answers," he said, pointing a finger at me a few inches from my bow tie. "You come to my office for a cup of coffee and you give me a name. You don't come and I'll find you. You can shove those Howard files. I'll find you, and what will I do?"

"Have me drip ground?" I tried.

"No, no," Shelly sobbed at my side.

"You got a sense of humor." Lipparini grinned. "Do I like a good sense of humor?"

"No," Moe said, blocking the door.

"He's right," said Lipparini, adjusting his jacket and turning to the mirror to admire himself.

I moved for the door, dragging Shelly behind me.

"One more thing," Lipparini said, looking at Shelly in the mirror. "I never want to see that fat beach ball again. He's got no heart. I don't like a guy who's got no heart."

Shelly almost fell, and it took all I had left in my arms and weak back to keep him up. Moe moved out of our way enough to let us pass, but just enough.

The Veronica Lake look-alike or real Veronica Lake was still there with her friends, but Shelly was no longer interested. He collapsed into the nearest lobby chair.

"Get up, Shel," I said.

"What did you get me into?" he said.

"You wanted to come, remember? Crash the party. Just like you and old Cal back in college. Let's get the hell out of here before Lipparini changes his mind."

Shelly got up slowly and followed me away from the ballroom, through a door, and into a hallway. There was a light at the end of the hallway. We followed it and found ourselves at the front entrance to Marty's. The guy at the door with the deep voice was talking to an elderly couple. He deserved an Oscar for covering his reaction when he saw us. He didn't even blink. We went through the door and out into the night.

Still dressed in our waiter suits, Shelly and I drove back downtown. "I'm not forgiving you for this, Toby," was the only thing he said.

I dropped him in front of the Farraday and watched him hurry toward his car in drooping black trousers and maroon jacket. He looked a little like Mickey Mouse from the rear.

It was getting late, and my choices were limited. I could go back to Mrs. Plaut's and suffer the slings and arrows of her comments on my uniform. Added to that would be the fact that I'd have to put the uniform on again in the morning.

Then I'd have to take the time to buy a new suit, either that or go through an investigation looking like Arthur Treacher.

The drive to Santa Monica was quiet, not too much traffic on the streets. Maybe people were waiting for the Jap raid, maybe they just didn't have gas. I listened to "That Brewster Boy" on the radio, felt good when Joey Brewster made the track team, and tried not to think about who was killing who and why.

There were no lights on at Anne's house when I pulled into the driveway, but I got out anyway and rang the bell. Then I rang again. It took about two minutes for someone to move inside. Then I heard the clop-clop of slippers coming toward me.

"Who is it?" Anne said.

"Me, Toby."

She opened the door. There was no light on inside.

"Air-raid warden came by earlier and told us to keep the lights . . ."

Then she laughed. She put her hand over her pink robe at the neck, started with a giggle, and began to laugh. I tried to think of the last time I'd heard her laugh. I think it was the night we saw *Bringing Up Baby* and she decided she wanted a divorce.

"That uniform," she said, holding her hand to her mouth. "You look like . . ."

"An usher," I helped her. "The emergency replacement bartender at Chasin's?"

"I'm sorry, Toby," she said.

"Can we laugh inside?" I asked, moving forward, and she stepped back.

She closed the door and switched on a small hall light. "I shouldn't be laughing," she said, "but I can't help it."

"Laugh," I said, holding my arms out so she could see me. I didn't think I looked all that funny, but I had the feeling she was letting a lot out that needed tears or laughter.

She held my arm, and her pink robe opened to show even more pink silk pajamas. "I'm sorry," she repeated.

"You already said that. When you finish, do you think we might find one of Ralph's old suits for me? We were about the same size."

The mention of Ralph almost turned the laughter to tears. There was a catch in her voice. She sobered a bit, but gave one more small laugh and said, "Come on."

I followed her up the stairs, where she hit another light switch and led me to a bedroom. A small reading light was on next to the unmade bed.

"I was reading," she explained. "The closet is there. Pick any suit you want."

There were about ten in the closet. More than half were eliminated. They were just too respectable for me. I'd look as if I'd borrowed a rich uncle's Sunday best. I found a light-weight blue suit and a matching striped tie. For good luck I took a white shirt from the shelf and turned to show my choice to Anne. She was sitting on the bed looking at me over her reading glasses, a book in her lap.

"Fine," she said. "Ralph always called that his go-to-the-movies suit."

Ralph had been a nice guy, but he never struck me as particularly clever, so I grunted. "One more request," I said. "Can I sleep here? I mean, you must have a guest room, servant's room. I could . . ."

"Yes," she said, holding the book in her lap to her breast. Her hair was less than perfect, almost perfect but not quite, a few dark strands were out of place and caught the light from the lamp. The book, I could see, was *Song of Bernadette*.

"I'll find the guest room," I said, moving to the door and looking back at her. There was something going on behind her eyes, something I recognized from long ago.

"Toby," she said, and I stopped. "You want to get into bed with me?"

"I'll think about it," I said, closed my eyes for a beat, and then in a wild rush threw Ralph's clothes in a nearby chair, pulled off my shoes, and began to fling waiter's clothes in all directions. When I had everything off but my undershorts, I looked at Anne, who had put down her book and glasses.

"You have more scars than I remembered," she said seriously.

"I've been through a lot since you last saw me with my shirt off," I said.

"Toby," she said seriously, still sitting up. "This is just one time. I don't want to be alone tonight. Tomorrow or the day after or the next day I'll pull myself together. You haven't changed. I haven't changed."

"But we have a history," I said, stepping forward.

"That we have," she said with a sigh, and she turned off the light.

8

It would have been a pretty good day if someone hadn't tried to kill me. But that came later.

In the morning, Anne told me to take a shower. I told her she was voluptuous. I also told her everything that had happened the day before, including why I had appeared at the door wearing a waiter's costume.

"I thought you did it just to cheer me up," she said across the breakfast table. I was wearing Ralph's go-to-the-movies suit, and she was dressed in a fittingly black widow's dress. Anjelica had appeared magically in the morning to serve toast and eggs with coffee. She was just a kid, but she knew how to keep a straight face. Her eyes didn't show the trace of a question about my being there in the morning in Ralph's suit.

"Anne," I said after my second cup of coffee and a third scrambled egg. I would have liked a bowl of Wheaties but she didn't have any cereal in the house. "How much did Ralph leave you?"

She looked at me with a counter question, changed her mind, and said, "I talked to our lawyer last night. Ralph mortgaged the house. There's not much in the bank, about two thousand. But his insurance will be enough to keep me comfortable until I decide what I want to do with my life."

"How comfortable?" I asked.

"One hundred and eighty thousand dollars," she said, biting her lower lip. "The company paid half the premiums.

It's standard. Working for an airline can be dangerous, even for executives."

We chatted about the weather, the beach litter, and a few mutual acquaintances from the past including Ruth and Phil. I knew Anne had meant last night as no more than two curious and once-familiar bodies comforting each other. Anne always meant what she said.

"I went to a psychiatrist last year," she said, offering me more coffee. I turned it down and she went on. "It's a new fad among the moderately well-to-do. He told me that I had married you because I wanted a little boy, and you satisfied that need. I wanted a child and couldn't have one, and you wanted a mother you had never really had."

I wanted to escape, but I shook my head politely and nibbled at the crust of my toast, which I didn't really want unless I could dip it into my coffee. I had controlled the urge, remembering Anne's morning look of veiled disgust when I had dipped, sopped, or sponged food in the past.

"I divorced you when I stopped wanting to play mother," she went on. "You wanted to keep playing baby. So, I married Ralph, who was . . ."

"A father figure," I said. "I could have saved you fifteen bucks a session."

"It was twenty-five," she said with a smile, "and your telling me wouldn't have made it true. It wasn't true until I told myself and believed it."

"Now you've got no father figure and you don't want to go back to the little boy. You're right. The little boy is pushing fifty and you outgrew him long ago. I understand. I don't like it, but I understand. Can I use the phone?"

There was a phone on the heavy wooden table by the door. I got up and went to it. I could have waited an hour, two maybe, but I didn't like this conversation.

"Hello, Shel," I said when he answered after the third ring.

"I'm not talking to you, Toby," he said. I could imagine him pursing his chubby lips.

"Don't talk to me then, Shel, just tell me if I've had any calls."

"Ha, how can I give you your messages if I'm not talking to you?"

"Shel, you've been talking to me to tell me you're not talking to me. Do I have any messages?"

"Your brother," he said. "He called. Toby, what am I going to do with a waiter's uniform? And what about my suit? That was a good suit. I've only got two suits."

"You can wear the waiter's costume to the next costume ball of the dental association," I said.

"The dental association doesn't have a costume ball. Maybe I could sell it to a costume shop?"

"Great idea, Shel," I said, wondering how much demand there was for a little fat waiter's costume. "If they won't take it, I'll buy you a new suit."

"Well . . ." he began and I said, "Good-bye, Shel. I'll talk to you later."

Anne was politely not listening or pretending that she wasn't. Her small smile betrayed her as she helped Anjelica clear the table. I called the Wilshire Station and asked for Captain Pevsner, who came on almost immediately.

"Toby," he said calmly. "You and that fat mouth-butcher went to see Monty Lipparini last night."

"Right, Phil. Is he complaining? I made a deal with him and—"

"He's not complaining," Phil said. "He won't complain to anybody any more. Monty Lipparini is dead. Your sloppy marksman gunned him down outside of Marty's Lounge in Beverly Hills. You better get in here."

"Phil, if I—"

"We've got four bodies, Toby. They're laying all over the county," he said too calmly. I could imagine Seidman in front of him, indicating that he should stay calm. "And Steve got the feeling talking to some of Lipparini's people that they'd like to have a little talk with you."

"Phil," I said earnestly. "Lipparini has a bodyguard. I don't know his name. Looks a little like a blown-up Moe Howard."

"Genette, Jerry Genette." He sighed. "He doesn't look anything like Moe Howard for chrissake. We questioned him. We're questioning everybody, even George Raft. This case is going to be all over the papers in the morning. Lipparini was rat shit, but he had a name. And by the way, Louis's lady friend says she never heard of him. I'm pulling him in, too. Get in here."

"Parkman," I tried.

"We're still looking," Phil answered. "Toby, get your ass in here. Meara wants you for this one. Lipparini's friends want you. And I want you. You take your choice."

"I try to find who killed everyone," I said. "That's my choice. And don't pull Louis in yet. I think Louis's lady friend might have an encounter with the Lord and decide to tell the truth."

"Get in—" he began and I hung up.

"Got to go," I said to Anne. "Meara is probably going to be here soon. A lot of people might be here soon. Tell them all whatever they want to hear, that I was here, that I was dressed like the Easter Bunny, the truth."

"Take care, Tobias Leo Pevsner," she said. She put down a dish and held her hand out to me. I took it, let it go reluctantly, said "*Adiós*" to Anjelica just like the Cisco Kid, and got the hell out of there as fast as I could go.

The morning was sunny, warm, and without a breeze. I got into my car and drove down the highway. A black sedan looked as if it might be tailing me, so I pulled into a circular driveway in front of a big beach house. I waved at the guy in shorts and sunglasses who came out to greet me and then pulled back onto the highway. The black sedan was far ahead and moving. Then I drove the last few hundred yards to the house I was looking for.

The house was about half a mile from Anne's and a little closer to the beach. It was a two-story wooden spider of a beach house built against the jagged hillside and supported by beams sunk into the sand and resting on rock below. A lot of these had been going up lately as Santa Monica became a place where the rich could spend a quiet weekend. The problem with the housing boom was the war. These unsteady sentinels would be the first to go in an invasion, but there were movie stars and people getting rich on selling guns and butter who didn't seem to worry about it or the possibility of the Pacific rolling over in anger to take the house and part of the hill some night when the water banshees were howling.

I stepped onto the wooden porch and looked down between the boards at the rocky beach twenty feet below. It made me nervous, but I kept going and knocked at the door.

The last two times Brenda Stallings had opened a door for me, I had wound up being seduced and shot by her and getting both of her husbands killed. I wasn't sure I wanted to cross this threshold again.

"I'm not married, Peters," she said. "There's no one here you can get killed."

She looked the same—cool, blonde, every hair perfect, her lips red and recently painted, her white dress a towelly material belted with a sash at her thin waist. She didn't look a minute over twenty-five and couldn't have been a year under thirty-eight. Brenda had been a wealthy society deb about seventeen years earlier. She had doubled for Harlow and then, after a short, successful film career, she had married a blackmailing actor named Harry Beaumont, who now resided in Roseland Cemetery. Her second husband, Richard Talbott, the star of *Captain Daring* and others of its ilk, had been knifed over a year ago by a nut I was trailing.

"Before you ask," she said, "Lynn is in New York and has in fact just married a producer several years older than I am and very interested in having a family in addition to the two he already has by his previous wives."

"Which means?" I asked, still standing on the porch.

"I may soon be a grandmother," she said. "Do I look like a grandmother?"

"Do I look like Robert Taylor?" I answered.

"There may be hope for you, Peters," she said with a twisted smile that didn't make her look less beautiful. "Come in."

"No guns," I said, stepping past her.

"No guns," she said, showing her hands.

White was her color. Her last two houses had been white on white on white, and this one was no exception. The carpet was white and the walls and furniture in the living room were white with tasteful blond wooden tables. Both of Brenda's previous husbands were honored by portraits on the wall. They seemed to be looking at each other and wondering what the hell they had done to deserve this.

There was a giant glass door facing the ocean. Beyond the sliding door was a porch and wooden steps leading down to the sand. The door was open, and the sound of rolling sea mixed with beach voices.

"Nice place," I said.

She shrugged, found a cigarette, lit it with an Oscar that had been turned into a lighter.

"Sand gets into the carpet, sand and salt air," she said, looking at the floor and then at me. "It looks as if you've had your share of sand and salt water in the last year or two."

"I don't weather very well," I said.

She looked at me with curiosity, folded her arms, showing scarlet fingernails, played with her cigarette.

"You want to know why I'm here?" I said with a smile.

"I assumed it wasn't just to talk about the good old days," she said, taking a white marble ashtray and wandering to the glass door. The light hit her from behind as she knew it would. It was perfect.

"Joe Louis," I said.

She laughed and said, "Of course. Are you going to get him maimed? Please try to bear in mind that I'm not married to him."

"You told the police you didn't know him," I reminded her.

"Peters, what would you tell the police in my place? My friends, or the only people I know on an extended basis, would think nothing of my friendship with Joe Louis. However, I don't want newspapers, magazines, and radio reporters camped on my door, and I don't want certain people with whom I plan to enter into business to have second thoughts about my viability as a partner."

She had begun pacing the room and smoking fiercely as she talked, which gave me some hope. I hadn't been thrown out, and she hadn't sat or stood calmly lying to me. Something was working at her, and I went for it.

"He's a decent guy," I said.

"He rides horses better than either of my two husbands, and he plays better golf than they did," she said. "And he excels in other areas, too. And you are right. He's a decent guy."

"The cops are trying to nail him for a murder down the beach," I said. I had been leaning against the wall, watching her stalk the room like a Persian cat. She walked nicely, glided across the carpet. "All you have to say is that he was staying with you and had a reason for being here."

She stopped and stared at me, putting out her cigarette and placing the ashtray on one of the wooden tables.

"Is that *all* I have to do?" she said, pursing her lips. "That and face the consequences?"

"The police will keep it out of the papers," I assured her, but she and I knew there was no guarantee of that.

"Shit," she said and stamped her foot and bit her lower lip. "Shit, shit, shit."

"And more shit," I agreed.

"I don't want to be a grandmother," she said.

"I don't want to be an ice fisherman in Alaska," I said, "but what choice do I have?"

Her shoulders sagged slightly. Everything she did was a pose. I wondered if she practiced in front of a mirror.

"I suppose in a sick kind of way I owe you something, Peters," she said, turning to me with her hands on her hips. It was the same pose, the same tone, and maybe even close to the same words she had shot at Warren William in *It Takes a Lady*.

"*It Takes a Lady*, 1936," I said.

"God no. It was *Vagabond From Genesis*, 1934," she said. "Can't help it. Too many rehearsals, too many directors. The only place I can be original is in bed. Do you remember?"

"It was a pool house and a deck chair, and you were stalling to keep me from finding your daughter," I said. "Yes, you were original, but now . . ."

"I'm stalling," she said. "Brenda Stallings. All right. Tell your policeman friends I'll verify that the Brown Bomber, the Detroit Dynamite, the Sepia Socker, the Champ was here because I invited him and all the rest. Do you think I might succeed in bribing the police to keep it quiet?"

"No," I said. "It would take care of a few of them but not enough to guarantee anything."

The phone rang, a white phone on the table near the white sofa.

"Then our visit is over?" she said, a trace of weariness touching the corners of her mouth.

"Over," I agreed between rings.

"You can let yourself out," she said, stepping toward the phone. "Does your back ever . . ." she said, pausing with her hand over the phone and looking at me.

"No, just a scar, a nice conversation piece when I show my body off for girls on the beach," I said.

"As I recall, you had plenty of scars on your body," she

said seductively, falling into her best-known character, Lucinda in *Belle of Forever*. Then, looking back at the insistent phone, she sighed. "A grandmother."

I left the room and headed for the door. Behind me I could hear her on the phone,

"Yes," she said, very businesslike. "I've just decided to do it, produce it myself, but as we agreed, only on condition that you direct and I star as both the mother and daughter."

I wanted to stay around and find out more about the project, but I had my own closets to open. I found a phone inside Schell's Grill on Wilshire in Santa Monica and called Phil to assure him that Brenda Stallings would be cooperative. He threatened me with vivid but not colorful images of what might happen to my body if I didn't turn myself in fast. I hung up on him for the second time that morning. My next call was to Jeremy. He didn't answer. I waited five minutes and called him again. This time he came on.

"I need a place to stay for a few days, Jeremy," I said. I explained the situation quickly while a woman with a crying little boy hovered behind me, wanting to use the phone.

Jeremy took about five seconds to think and came up with: "I just purchased a court complex. Six one-room apartments in Burbank just off Olive I'm renovating now. No tenants. The units are furnished, though the furniture will have to be changed. It needs work."

"I'm not fussy," I said. "Just desperate."

The woman waiting for the phone picked up her kid to show me how much of a burden he was and to get his weeping closer to my ear. Jeremy gave me the address and concluded by saying, "Apartment number six has a window that won't lock. You can go through it. I'll come by to see you before dark with some supplies and books."

"Thanks, Jeremy," I said and hung up.

The woman almost hit me with the wailing kid, but I sidestepped like a ranking bantamweight and went for the door.

Twenty minutes later I pulled into the parking space for the Ocean Breeze Apartments in Burbank. It was about a mile or two from Warners and just off Olive. It looked to me as if it were the shame of the neighborhood and needed a lot more than renovation if it was to hold its own with the nearby single-family homes big enough to have brick walls or iron fences.

I climbed over the broken wire mesh put up to keep kids out. Actually it wouldn't keep any self-respecting nine-year-old out, though it would let them know they weren't supposed to try. The Ocean Breeze was far enough away from traffic so that it wasn't likely any bums might find the place and camp in it while Jeremy hammered, cleaned, and attempted to save the crumbling wreck.

The apartments were in a horseshoe around a pond. The pond wasn't exactly empty. There were a few beer bottles and a mat of decaying grass in it, and a lemon tree gone wild stood on its bank. The lemons were ripe, and a bluebird was chirping on a branch.

Apartment number six was exactly in the middle of the curve of the horseshoe. There were only two windows facing the courtyard. I found the one with the broken lock, climbed in, and opened the front door to let a little light in and a little bad air out. Then I pulled up the shades. The room wasn't as bad as I had feared. Then again, it wasn't as good as I had hoped. I had enough cash to change my mind and go to a hotel, but with both the police and the Lipparini mob looking for me even a false name might not be enough.

The furniture in number six wasn't too dusty but it was old. It looked like it had all been junked from my parents' living room back in 1927. There was a tiny, dark alcove with a refrigerator. I checked it. It was warm and smelled like mildew. Then I checked the second room. There was a bed, just a spring and mattress, both too soft. There was also a small shower stall in the corner covered by an olive drab canvas curtain. I tried the light switch. No electricity. I tried the shower. The water sputtered and spat out in a brown stream. I let it run until it turned tan and then slightly clear. Having explored the place, I sat on the bed and tried to think about what the hell I was going to do next. The only thing I came up with was a plan to have lunch in a few hours.

I found a dirty glass pitcher in a cupboard next to the refrigerator, rinsed it out, picked five lemons from the tree, and tried to make lemonade. I dragged a wooden chair out into the courtyard and sat drinking warm sugarless lemonade at the dry pond while I pondered who was killing who and why. The only names I could come up with were Jerry Genette, who I still thought fondly of as Moe Howard; Al Parkman; and Anne. I couldn't think of any reason, at least not a good one, why Genette or Parkman would kill Ralph, Mush, Silvio, and Lipparini, but that didn't mean they didn't have reasons. I just didn't know them. Anne had the best reason, money, but I knew she hadn't done it. And, of course, it could have been any one of several hundred thousand people. Hell, none of the murders were related, and maybe we were dealing with three different killers. Maybe it was infectious murder, a record-book coincidence.

I don't know what time Jeremy showed up. I had taken off Ralph's shirt and jacket and dozed off in the chair in the shade of the lemon tree. When I saw him climbing over the wire mesh, I automatically checked my old man's watch, which told me it was nine, which it surely was not. Jeremy was wearing a brown windbreaker and carrying a large paper bag.

"You see the possibilities here, Toby," he said, his well-polished bald pate gleaming in the late afternoon sun. "Some paint, new furnishings, fresh water in the pond and some fish, a few new trees and a new name. What do you think would be a good name? I've been considering Fidelia's Garden: -

"As withered weed through cruel winterstine,
That feels the warmth of sunny beam's reflection

Lifts up his head, that did before decline
And gins to spead his leaf before the fair sunshine."

"Did you write that or Byron?" I asked, knowing Jeremy's two favorite poets.

"Edmund Spenser," he said. "Generally I find him too elusive and pastoral, but he inspires me when I'm faced with a clean-up job like this. Byron is not to be read when one has work to do, but Spenser is fine. I brought you a book."

He reached into the paper bag and handed me a hardcover copy of *As William James Said: A Treasury of His Work*.

"Thanks, Jeremy," I said. "I'd probably be up all night reading it if there were electricity."

Jeremy's hand went back into the bag and came out with a metal Army lamp. "I have extra batteries," he said, patting the bag. "I've also brought you a towel, a bit of food, and a newspaper."

I got out of my chair, thanked him, and led him into number six.

"How's the book give-away coming?" I asked politely, putting the paper bag and lamp down on the counter in the alcove.

"*Doves of a Winter Night* is off to a good start," Jeremy said. "Alice and I have a meeting with a member of the Whittier school board tomorrow. I'm hoping we can be persuasive."

If the Whittier school board member was less than seven feet tall and weighed under three hundred, Alice and Jeremy would surely be persuasive.

"Sounds good," I said.

We talked for about half an hour before Jeremy said he had to leave. He was meeting Alice for a strategy session on how to present their book to the board member.

"One final thing," he said, walking to the door. "I would like your advice. Max Edelstein, the wrestling promoter, has asked me to come out of retirement for an exhibition to raise money for Armed Forces Relief. He wants me to read a few poems and then go two minutes each with volunteer servicemen. I'm well aware that it is a gimmick. The wrestling doesn't bother me, but I don't want my poetry demeaned."

"Don't read your own poetry," I said. "Read some of your favorites."

"I like that," he said. "No one would have the temerity to laugh at Lord Byron."

"Not with you around," I agreed. "Thanks for the package, Jeremy."

"Try not to do anything foolish, Toby," he said. "Each year, each moment we become a little more frail of body and, if we're fortunate, a little more strong of spirit."

"I'll be careful, Jeremy," I said.

When he was gone, I tested the lamp. It worked. I didn't plan to sit around reading William James. I had a feeling William was not Frank and Jesse's brother, but the lamp would be nice to have. I also found soap, a towel, a loaf of bread, a pound of sliced salami, some mustard, and a knife, along with a quart of milk in a paper carton. I didn't like cartons. The wax kept coming off in the milk. I made a sandwich, washed it down with milk, and switched on the lamp. The sun was going down. I'd wasted the whole damn day with no plan.

The best thing I could come up with was a trip to Parkman's house. He wasn't as high on my list of suspects as he was on Phil's, but he was the one I could most easily go after. Jerry Genette wouldn't need going after. He would be coming for me.

I went into the bedroom carrying the lantern, took off my clothes, and turned on the shower. There was no heater, but the water came out reasonably warm. I showered and sang "Ramona" in the darkening room. The water pelted my puffed cheek pleasantly.

While I was rubbing myself with soap, the beam of a car headlight slashed across the window near my head. I kept

singing while somewhere down deep I figured out what was
outside that window. It was the Ocean Breeze parking lot.
Maybe Jeremy was coming back or someone was lost. With
the water bouncing off my head, I opened the window a little
to take a look and heard the bullet crack past my right eye
and into the wall behind me. I crouched down, almost slip-
ping. The next two bullets cracked through the window,
spraying glass all over the shower and against the canvas
shower curtain.

All the killer had to do now, if that's who it was, was to
walk over to the window and shoot at the cowering, soapy
creature below him. I didn't have a lot of choices. I rolled out
of the showe.. I didn't stop to turn off the water. I wasn't sure
if I had stepped on any glass, but I didn't have time to check.
My .38 was in the glove compartment of my car outside.
There was nothing I could see that would be a reasonable
weapon against a gun, even one fired by the Elmer Fudd
marks·nan outside.

While I considered whether to grab my pants and go for
the door, I heard something above the sound of the shower,
and I didn't like what I heard. The front door of the two-
room apartment was pushed open with a *screek.* Since there
was only one window in the room, I went back into the
shower and crawled through it, grabbing the wet towel as I
scrambled. This time I knew I had cut my foot on a shard of
glass. It didn't feel too bad. A bullet in my wet skin would
have been worse. I rolled naked on the dirt drive, looked
around, and decided what I could and could not do. I couldn't
get into my car and drive away. My keys were in my pants
pocket. I couldn't even get my .38. The car was locked. I
could break the window and try for the gun, but that would
mean looking for a rock and making a lot of noise, by which
time I could be dodging bullets.

There was a black sedan, the killer's, parked next to my
Ford, but I didn't think there was much chance of the key
being in it. So I ran for a clump of nearby bushes, my towel

flying behind me. I heard the shower turn off behind me as I reached the nearest bush and kneeled behind it. The night was turning cool. I wrapped the wet towel around my waist and huddled like an ape or Bill Dickey waiting for the next pitch. I tried to look back through the bush without panting too hard.

A figure appeared in the window, but I couldn't make it out clearly. It was too dark outside, and the lantern inside didn't penetrate the canvas shower curtain. There was no place to run, and I didn't think I could make it over the wooden fence behind me, so I shivered, watched, and waited.

Inside the room I could hear glass kicked around and the sound of something, cloth tearing. The killer said or cried something and then was quiet. My teeth began to chatter, but I didn't move, and then a minute later I saw the figure come back around the building and head toward the sedan. The sky was cloudy, and since there were no lights close by, I still couldn't see him or her. I thought the figure was wearing a wool cap and a pea coat, but I also knew I might simply be seeing what I wanted to see, what Gunther had said the guy who had come out of Reed's with Parkman had been wearing.

The killer walked to the car, and the walk looked familiar. The killer looked around, gun in hand, and got in the car.

"Hurry, hurry you bastard," I urged quietly. "I'm freezing."

The car backed up slowly, reluctantly, and drove off. I wanted to run for the apartment, but I waited and counted. When I hit two hundred the car reappeared, its lights out, moving slowly into the Ocean Breeze Apartments parking lot. It lingered, and the killer turned on the car lights, got out, watched, listened, and made a mistake. The figure moved forward and stepped into the right headlight beam, the bright light slashing ghostly over a familiar face.

Still I didn't move. About twenty seconds later the killer gave up, got in the car, and drove off. I didn't think the car would come back. It was possible, but it didn't make sense to keep this up all night. My killer would feel reasonably safe and wait for another chance. Of course, I could have been wrong. It was not beyond my experience to be wrong.

I moved cautiously in a Groucho crouch, holding the towel around my waist, and dashed behind my car. I waited for about twenty seconds more and began to make my way along the wall, stepping on things I didn't want to think about. Around the building and inside the courtyard I still moved slowly, in shadows, stopping to listen for a returning car and trying to control my own chattering teeth and heavy breathing. Inside room six the lamp was still on.

I moved to the bedroom and put on my underpants and trousers. There is something about dying naked that scares the hell out of me. Dying with clothes on isn't much better. I couldn't put on the jacket. The killer had torn it into four or five pieces and I thought I knew why. I gathered what I had to gather, turned off the lamp, and got the hell out of the Ocean Breeze. When I got to my car, I opened the glove compartment and got my gun out. I drove with it in my lap.

There was no going back to Anne's. The killer had followed me from there and had waited for night to take a shot at me. I tried to imagine a shoot-out between the two of us. I was probably a slightly better shot than the person who was coming for me, but just slightly. At five feet I knew I could hit Mush and Silvio lying on the floor. It had been a problem for the killer. I didn't know how close the killer had been when Lipparini was gunned down.

There were no lights on at Doc Hodgdon's house when I pulled up in front of it a little before eleven, at least none that I could see from the street. It was a frame house, the first floor of which Doc Hodgdon had converted to office space for his orthopedic practice in 1919. They didn't call it orthopedics in 1919. He still didn't. He was a specialist in backs and bones. I had met Doc six years earlier at the YMCA, and we had started playing handball somewhat regularly. He was old when I met him. Six years later I had still never managed to beat him. He wasn't fast, but he wasn't slow either. He beat me on smarts and a strong right hand. Maybe the hand came with the orthopedic business.

I limped up the walk and stairs and knocked. Hodgdon's secretary-receptionist Myra and I had clashed a couple of times, and I was hoping she wouldn't be working late, trying to reconstruct a skeleton. I rang the bell and waited, peering through the small square window in the door. A light came on somewhere and got brighter when a door deep inside the house opened. Then I saw Hodgdon walking to the door and flipping on the light.

"I have a feeling this isn't a social call," Hodgdon said, looking at me. He was wearing a red flannel shirt. His gray hair was curly and looked as if he had just rinsed it in Prell.

"Repairs," I said. "Can I come in? I can pay the bill this time."

We crossed the room to his office. He switched on the light and turned to examine me. "Toby," he said tolerantly. "The county hospital has an emergency room for things like this. If your back is the problem, however, we can wait till morning after I give you a few pills."

"Can't go to the hospital," I said. "The good guys and the bad guys are looking for me."

He shook his head and motioned for me to sit on the examining table. Then he looked at my face. "How'd you get that?" he said, looking for something to use on my face, something I feared would feel like knives dipped in frozen lime juice.

"Someone was trying to teach me to read," I explained, "but I didn't learn fast enough."

"When we speak cryptically, we run the risk of being treated cryptically," he said, pouring something from a bottle onto a piece of white cloth he extracted from a jar.

"I'll try to remember that," I said as he applied the compress to my face. *"Yigh,"* I said or shouted.

"That's what they all say," he whispered. "But it doesn't change the situation. You didn't just get that. It should have been cleaned at least twenty-four hours ago."

There was an electric tingling across the side of my face for the count of four or five and then no feeling at all.

"Didn't come about my face, Doc," I said.

He looked at me, resurveying my limbs, and said, "Are you going to tell me or do I guess. If I guess, I'm afraid you are going to walk out of here with a lobotomy, which ultimately may be the best thing for you. Did this teacher of yours happen to work on your skull?"

"A little," I said. "But that's not it. My foot's cut, and I can't sit around waiting for it to heal. I've got a killer to catch." With clenched teeth I took off my shoe and sock, which stuck to the wound.

"Well," he said, motioning me back on the table so he could prop up my leg and get a better look. "Most of my patients don't have reasons as pressing or colorful as yours for being treated quickly. My guess is you decided to hop around on ground glass."

"It was either that or get shot," I explained.

"Of course," he said, putting his nose down to the wound and lifting my foot.

I giggled. "You're tickling," I explained.

"I'm surprised you have any sensation in the bottom of that foot. I don't think you're going to be playing handball for a month or two, but I'll be open to modifying that diagnosis. I've witnessed your recuperative powers before. Hold still and think about the sound of rain, a woman of whom you are particularly fond, or a story you want to recall. There will, I'm afraid, be some pain connected with this."

I thought about Anne, my father's grocery in Glendale, and tried to recall the plot of a movie I'd seen a few years ago with James Cagney as a gangster who became a dancer, or maybe he was a boxer who became a dancer, or maybe I was thinking of two different James Cagney movies or maybe I was thinking about George Raft. No, I was thinking about the pain in the bottom of my foot as Doc Hodgdon worked to remove pieces of glass and dirt and to clean it out with corrosive liquids.

"Done in a few more minutes," he said.

I wasn't looking. My eyes wandered around the little room and rested on the painting on the wall, a group of peasants in some village maybe a hundred years ago. They were gathered around a well in what looked like a town square, watching a young woman in ragged dress drawing water into a big, washed-out green vase.

"Nice picture," I said without quite opening my mouth.

"Wife liked it," he said, not looking up but finding some new tool to probe my underfoot. "I think she thought she looked like the girl."

"Did she?"

"I thought so," he said. "That's why it's still there. You're done. But don't get down. I assume you were serious about having to find a murderer."

"I was serious," I said as seriously as I could.

"I put some sutures in the foot. It's going to throb, but that's not a new experience for you. I'll put on a thin absorbent bandage and plenty of tape. You may be all right, but I doubt it."

"Thanks, Doc," I said as he applied the tape.

"I know your game, Peters," he said, stepping back to examine his work. "Destroy your body so I'll take pity on you. Eventually, time will take its toll on me and work with pity on your side, and I'll be ripe for you to win a handball game."

"That's the plan," I agreed, reaching down to put my

sock back on. There was some pain, but it was tolerable. Getting the shoe on was a bit tougher.

"Foot's going to swell," he said, gathering his tools and moving to the small sink in the corner to clean them. "Maybe a lot. Maybe not so much. Might have some trouble getting a shoe on, not to mention walking. I am, however, aware of the extremes humans can tolerate if motivated. A primary problem with patients is that they know they're sick. They give themselves conventional time to recover. Something like the job I just did on you could keep a sensible person who knew the rules off his feet for a week at least. You could ruin the sympathy racket, Toby."

He took the washed instruments and put them in a steel container about the size of a breadbox. A piece of adhesive was stuck to the box and in pencil on the adhesive was written *For sterilization.* Maybe some day I would drag Shelly over here.

"A beer?" he said, turning his back to me.

"Sounds just fine," I said.

"Well, hobble after me and we'll open some bottles."

After a few bottles of Goebels beer at the kitchen table, I said, "Well, aren't you going to give me the warning? My body can't take this kind of abuse. I won't feel right unless I hear it."

"Why?"

"Because you're right. I should stop, but some people are surgeons, some telephone repairmen, some detectives who meet some not-very-nice people."

Hodgdon took a drink of beer from the tall glass and watched me do the same before he spoke. "Too late to change you," he said. "You only change the very young because you've got things going for you like fear and authority and their flexibility. You can change the old too sometimes because they too get frightened, but you are a pterodactyl, a creature who should have been trapped in a tar pit a millenium ago. You fly and hunt and don't think about your own extinction."

He poured himself another beer and I said, "Doc, I think you are just a bit drunk."

"I had a few beers before you got here," he admitted, holding his glass up to examine the foam, slowly searching for the bottom of the glass. "These two beers with you are two over my limit. I'm not a drinking man."

We sat talking about his son in Indianapolis, who was also a doctor, and his daughter, who had married an insurance salesman in Chicago.

"Jean and the kids are going to visit me this summer," he said. "Alex, her husband, doesn't want them to come. The Japanese might be here any day. Tojo landing up in Monterey and running down here swinging his sword. Some people live frightened lives, Peters."

"I guess he's just worrying about his family," I said.

"World's not big enough to hide in anymore," Hodgdon said, reaching over to pour me more beer. "You go out the door in the morning and you run the risk of getting your lumbar turned to chalk by a delivery truck. No, it's better to dance occassionally on broken glass than to stay away from bottles."

We finished about an hour later, and I tried to pay him twenty bucks for the treatment.

"Make it five," he said. "That will satisfy your honor and pay my expenses, even cover the beer."

Armed with a bottle of pain pills and a warm feeling for even my enemies, I said good-bye to Doc Hodgdon and went back to my car. I didn't remember my foot hurt till I was almost a block away.

I drove slowly back to Mrs. Plaut's boarding house, making extra turns, checking for headlights behind me. I thought I had gotten rid of that sedan earlier in the day, but I had been almost dead wrong. I didn't want to be wrong again.

I parked almost two blocks away from the boarding house, in the lot of the Church of Tomorrow. Mrs. Plaut was a member in good standing. That might count for something in heaven when they doled out punishment for those who parked near the church and didn't go in.

There was no black sedan on Heliotrope as I walked on the opposite side of the street, my .38 bulging in my pants pocket. I climbed over the white wooden railing of the boarding house, eased through the shadows to the door, and went in.

Mrs. Plaut caught me before I had taken two steps.

"Mr. Peelers, you look worse than Custer," she said, her hand going to the throat of her brown Victorian dress.

"I was almost General Custer," I admitted. "Trapped at the Battle of Ocean Breeze."

"My great Uncle Kenan Waltz was at the Little Big Horn," she said, shaking her head at me.

"I know," I reminded her. "I read the chapter."

"Wait," she said and scurried back into her room. I looked back at the door, my hand on the gun, and waited. She appeared with a dark, red bottle and a small tube along with a roll of gauze.

"Your foot, in case you have not noticed, is bleeding," she said, handing me the bottle, tube, and gauze. I tried to take it with one hand.

"You can let your gun alone for a second," she said. "I will not shoot you, and the people who have been looking for you are not present. It pains me to say this, Mr. Peelers, but many of those with whom you associate are most unsavory, most unsavory."

"I know," I agreed. "It's part of the business."

"It's probably part of your business," she mused. "Though I can't imagine why people would get so upset with an exterminator that you would need a pistol. You can explain it when time permits. Meanwhile, I insist that you do not shoot anyone in here tonight, or for that matter, at any time in the future. If they shoot you, that is another matter, one quite outside of your control."

"Thanks, Mrs. Plaut," I said, hobbling to the stairs.

"Least you could do is say thanks," she said.

I wanted to shout thanks to her, but couldn't risk it. Police, mobsters, and a killer might be outside. With luck they might all bump into each other and eliminate the competition for my scalp.

Gunther was waiting for me at the top of the stairs. My foot was hurting now from glass, gravel, medical treatment, and the unknown pieces of past lives of the Ocean Breeze Apartments.

"Toby," he whispered, "many have been looking for you."

"I know, Gunther," I said. "One of them found me."

"Can I help?" he said.

"I'm going into my room, where I'm going to take care of some cuts and bruises," I said, "which might be a bit of trouble since I don't want to turn my light on. Then I am going to try to get a few hours rest."

I took the pistol out of my pocket and handed it to Gunther. It filled both of his hands.

"If you can read a book out here with the gun handy, I'd appreciate it. You can hear anyone coming up the stairs."

"And what shall I do?" he asked seriously.

"With the exception of Mrs. Plaut, Mr. Hill, Mr. Stanton, and the Wycoff sisters, all of whom live here, and the possible exception of Joe Louis and the President of the United States, shoot any son of a bitch who comes up those stairs."

"If it is necessary," Gunther said seriously.

"Good," I said. "We'll talk all about it in the morning."

I went into my room, hoping no one was hiding in one of the few available corners. I didn't sense anyone. I propped a chair under the doornob, stripped off my clothes, and took off my shoes. It hurt to take off my right shoe. My sock stuck to the tape and I held back a grunt of pain as I pulled it off. Mrs. Plaut hadn't told me whether I was supposed to put the bottle of red liquid on the cut or drink it. I opened the bottle and smelled it. Then I tasted it. It was cherry-flavored and alcoholic. I took a drink. It tasted like dinosaur piss, but it felt like it was doing its job. I untaped my foot and used the stuff in the tube on the stitches, and, by the little light from the window, I wrapped the gauze back around the cut and my foot, tying it clumsily before sinking back on my mattress. Outside the door I had heard Gunther pull a chair out of his room and drag it in front of my door.

I didn't have a hell of a lot of faith in Gunther's ability as a gunfighter. I didn't even know if he could pull the trigger with both hands. My gun purposely didn't have a loose trigger. It was, I always thought, better to struggle to get off a shot than to accidentally blow off my own kneecap.

Sleep came easily, sleep and dreams. The killer came running up the beach in front of Anne's house, keeping pace with Joe Louis. They jogged along in slow motion toward me, and I stood there waiting. I wanted to run, but my legs were locked, heavy, unreal. The killer had a gun, but Joe Louis didn't seem to notice or didn't care.

I tried to shout to the Champ to ask him to help, to stop the killer, but nothing came out of my mouth. Then I figured out what to do. I had to wake up before the killer got close enough to shoot. It was simple. I told myself to wake up, but it didn't work. I strained to wake up, pleaded with myself to wake up, shouted at myself to wake up, and then my eyes did come open. I sat up heavily as the door to my room scraped open and the chair I had put under the knob fell with a clatter.

Gunther stood over me, concern on his face. "Toby, you screamed," he said, putting the pistol down.

Daylight was coming through the window and I knew I

had slept and that Gunther had sat all night outside my door with the gun in his lap.

"I'm all right," I said dryly. "A bad dream."

On the floor next to the mattress was a strange stain in the rug. It was white and looked to me vaguely like a skull. At first I thought it was some warning given by the killer, who had crept in while I slept, but then I realized that I had made the stain the night before in the dark when I tried to bandage my foot. The magic ointment had burned a reminder to me of what I had to do next.

I told Gunther the situation and gave him the name of the killer in case something happened to me.

"I do not understand," he said when I told him. "Why, Toby? In literature I encounter great reasonableness. People behave according to their established characteristics. If they have a deviation from what we feel is within the realm of their behavior, we say the literature is unreal, and yet we frequently encounter real people who contradict expected behavior: sober people who tell a funny joke, gentle people who do violence."

"I guess that's the difference between literature and life," I said, zipping up an old blue baseball jacket and trying to find a way of comfortably hiding my pistol under it. "In literature we expect people to be real. Real people don't have to worry about things like that."

There were dark sags under Gunther's small eyes as he nodded sadly.

"Get some sleep, Gunther," I said. "Maybe everything will be wrapped up tonight and we can have that dinner."

"Be—"

"—very careful," I finished. "I will."

I went out on the landing to the pay phone and placed my call. Anne thought my questions were a bit wacky and my excuses for asking them a bit lame, but she went along and gave me the answers. She also told me that I had missed Meara when I left her house by about five minutes.

Before she could press me for more information, I told her I had to run, and hung up. I didn't have information yet, just an answer.

I made no attempt to be quiet going down the stairs with my gun tucked awkwardly into my pocket and the bottle in my hand. I knocked at Mrs. Plaut's door. No answer. I knocked again. Still no answer but the chirping of Sweet Alice. I went back through the house, crossed the kitchen, and ducked out the back door to the garage, where I found Mrs. Plaut working on her car. She sensed rather than heard me, and looked up. There was a smudge of grease on her nose and cheek.

"Returning your medicine," I said, holding out the bottle and tube. "It helped."

"Are you going out to shoot someone?" she said, nodding at the bulge under my jacket.

"I hope not," I said.

"You may call it rot in your youth," she said angrily. "I call it good sense. The days a man could take the law into his hands are past. It's not like it was when my grandfather defended the drugstore."

"Not like it at all," I agreed.

"Mr. Plaut's auto-mobile is almost ready," she said proudly. She had been working on it for years, learning her skills from outdated manuals and library books.

"I plan to take frequent excursions to points not very distant that figure heavily in my family history," she went on seriously.

"It will provide much needed detail," I said, though the book she had been working on would drown all the great poets in description.

"Birds are a comfort, but they can also be a responsibility," she added from nowhere.

"They are and can be," I agreed.

"But not as much as dogs."

"Not as much as dogs." I nodded knowingly, not knowing whether we were talking about comfort or responsibility or what.

I knew the audience was ended when Mrs. Plaut rubbed her hands on her oversized overalls and plunged back under the hood of the car. I went around the garage, down the alleyway, and checked the street before crossing over to the church's parking lot, where my car was standing alone and unticketed.

I got in, took a deep breath, and reached over to turn on the ignition. Before I could turn the key, I felt the cool metal of a pistol barrel against my neck.

9

"I'm really not a bad guy," Meara said behind me, easing up on the pressure against my neck now that I knew he was there.

"I never thought you were," I said amiably.

"Sure," he said with a puff of air from his red cheeks. "You say that now when I have a gun on you, but what would you say if I put it away?"

"Good-bye," I tried.

I watched him shift to a more comfortable position and try to straighten his badly rumpled suit.

"You're a funny guy, Peters," he said. "I mean it. Damn, it's uncomfortable back here. You ever think of cleaning this thing out? You got books, empty pop bottles, and who knows what kind of shit."

"Sorry," I said, watching his pink face in the rearview mirror. "You were saying you're not a bad guy."

"Right, right," he agreed. "Thanks. I mean I considered placing the barrel of this weapon against your head a few times when you got in. I've been sitting here for four hours thinking about just what I would do. Couldn't come up with anything. If I hadn't dozed off I'd probably be in a really bad mood. But the sleep helped."

"Good morning."

"God," he said, rubbing his nose and the stubble on his face. "I could use something to eat."

"You want me to drive you to a restaurant or take you up

to my room for breakfast? I've got some Shreddies and a few eggs and coffee."

"No thanks," he said. "My car is around the corner. I'll get something when we're done. You know, you're wanted for questioning in the murder last night. You want to guess who died?"

"Lipparini," I said.

"Lipparini," he repeated. "Personally, I don't care if you take out Lipparini, those two shits at the gym. That's on your own time. I'm still working the Ralph Howard murder. And I want something from you."

"The Negro on the beach," I said.

"Parkman," he groaned. "I thought you were smart. I don't want the nigger anymore. Your captain brother covered that up with a neat little report. I figure Parkman for all of it, and that's the fella I want."

"What if he didn't do it?"

He shrugged indifferently. "I'll know that after I have a little talk with him. You give him to me, or we can finish our little talk back at the library. Better than that. I can turn you over to Lipparini's friends."

Someone came out of the church, a man who might have been the bishop or reverend or whatever he was called. He looked at me and Meara through the front window of the car. The man was tall and distinguished-looking. He looked as if he might come over and find out what the devil we were doing there, but Meara held up his gun so the man could see it and the good Samaritan changed his mind. Our souls could wait and he could, for the moment, forgive our trespasses.

"You wouldn't turn me over to Lipparini's friends," I said. "You're a lot of things, Meara, but I can't see you dealing with the bandits."

"Yeah," he said, looking out the window and chewing on his thumb. "I told you I was a nice guy."

"You said you weren't a bad guy," I reminded him.

"That's not the same thing. Let's deal. I turn Parkman over to you by tomorrow morning at the latest, or I come in myself and you can finish showing me the book of the month."

He thought about it. I could tell he was thinking by the way he looked back at my neck and tapped the barrel of the pistol against his teeth.

"I don't know a hell of a lot about you, Peters, but I know you stand up on your word."

"It's all I've got to sell," I agreed.

"Naw, you've got a big mouth and a hard head," he said. "Tomorrow morning at the latest. I'll be at my desk or Belleforte will. If both of us are in the can or at lunch, you keep calling. I don't want your brother to have Parkman, not no way, not no time."

"You want to shake on it?" I offered.

Meara put his gun into his shoulder holster, looked at his right palm, and decided to keep his hand on his side of the seat. "Eat shit," he said, getting out of the car and slamming the door.

I rolled down my window and grinned at him. "You really hold your own, Meara. 'Eat shit.' I'll have to remember that one."

As I started the car, Meara began to kick the rear fender. His kicking brought the reverend to the window of the church nearest us. I backed out fast, leaving Meara and the man of God to work it out. I knew about where I was going, and I had enough gas to get there. I reached over, put the .38 in the glove compartment, and drove.

The radio told me that the RAF had hit Nazi bases in northern France and that Ma Perkins was having a problem with her daughter; and the day looked pleasant. One of the things I missed on the radio since the war started was the weather reports. The newspapers didn't tell you what was going to happen, the radio didn't tell you. Walter Winchell said the reason was to keep vital information from the enemy. If the Japanese didn't have their own weatherman, we had nothing to worry about.

I took Long Beach Boulevard to Ocean Boulevard and headed south down past Huntington Beach and Costa Mesa. It took a few minutes for me to get lost in the San Joaquin Hills, looking for Pedras Blancas. I overshot it and got directions back at a gas station on Laguna Canyon Road. It was a little after noon. I wasn't hungry, but my back was stiff and I had mixed feelings about what I was going to do.

I bought a couple of Whiz candy bars and a bottle of Pepsi from the guy at the gas station and talked to him for a while about business and the drop in tourist trade since the war. He was about sixty, weathered like a yucca tree, and had three sons in the war. He pointed out the service flag with three stars in the window of his gas station.

When I finally got to Pedras Blancas, I found a small all-purpose store with a gas pump and a counter with six stools. I asked the old woman in the store for directions and got back in the car.

There were two ways up to where I was going. I could drive the narrow road to the top of the hill, or I could climb through the woods on the slope and approach the cabin from the rear. I decided to pull into a clump of trees and make my way up the slope. If I drove up the road, chances were good I'd have a few bullet holes in my windshield and maybe in my head.

It was the hottest part of the day, and the sun was having a good time, but my throbbing right foot wasn't in the mood. The gun in my pocket, the steepness of the hill, and my sore foot put me in a bad mood. I shifted the gun to my belt and kept going, making as little noise as I could and using shrubs and tree trunks to keep from falling. If the person I was looking for wasn't there, I'd have some time to catch my breath, get into the cabin, rest my foot, and wait—that is, if I had picked the right place. I could figure that out when I got to the cabin.

When I got to the top of the hill, I stood behind a tree catching my breath. I was in reasonably good shape. I didn't smoke and seldom had more than a beer, preferably a Falstaff. I worked out at the YMCA on Hope Street two or three times a week, meaning I played handball with Doc Hodgdon and I punched a bag that didn't punch back.

It was the right place. I could tell by the black sedan in front of the cabin when I finally got to the top of the hill. Not only was it the right place, but the person I'd come for was here or the car wouldn't be. The big problem was the clearing around the cabin. The cabin sat in the middle of that grassy clearing. Three metal garbage cans sat next to the house, the only possible cover. A raccoon was pawing at one of the cans, trying to figure a way to get it open.

There were windows on all four sides of the cabin. It wasn't much of a house, but it was enough, two sections, real sanded log with an enclosed and covered patio on one side, a comfortable little cabin. Maybe I wouldn't be seen. No reason to assume I'd be seen. I crouched, working my way around, and moved toward the cabin from behind. My sore foot made itself known. It had complained to me all the way up the hill, but I had taken that slowly. Now I was hurrying and my foot didn't like it. The raccoon heard me coming, got scared, pushed against the garbage can, and knocked it over. I kept coming as I heard the cabin door open. I almost made it.

The killer came around the side of the house in a red flannel shirt and dark trousers, spotted the raccoon running for the trees and me slouching toward the rear of the house. He shot just as I pushed against the side of the cabin, out of sight. He shot again, even though he couldn't see me anymore, and hit the cabin.

"I've got a gun," I said.

"I've got a gun," he said.

"What now?" I asked.

"I don't know," he said. "I suppose I have to try to kill you."

The raccoon was rustling the brush as he ambled away, and I tried to think of another way of settling the situation.

"You could put down the gun and come back with me," I tried. "Hell, you might wind up getting shot here and not me."

"I think that would be better than going back," he said. I tried to think of another argument, but I had to agree with him. In his place, I'd see it the same way. The difference was that I'd never be in his place.

Instead of talking, I moved as quietly as I could around the cabin, away from him. I rounded the building and moved to the front. I peeked around the corner. He wasn't there. Beyond the sedan I could see the road leading up the hill. I tried to find a dry place on my clothes to wipe my sweating palm and get a better grip on my gun. My pants weren't too bad.

With my gun in front of me, I stepped out in front of the cabin and shuffled across the front of the building to the side, where I could see him if he were still standing where he had been. He wasn't there. My right foot was numb and my left was on its own. A shot hit the cabin above me, and a second broke the nearby window. I turned and fired in the direction I'd just come. He was standing there, and I thought for a second that I'd hit him, but he raised his gun and took two more shots. The first ran a dark fingerline in the gravel in front of me. The second raced into the woods.

I flattened myself against the wall, held my breath, and took aim while he shot again. His shot was so far off it pinged against the fender of the black sedan. My shot caught the outside of the shoe on his left foot. It made him jump back.

"We're both god-awful at this," I said. "But I think I'm a little better than you are. For chrissake, give it up."

He dashed through the door into the cabin and I tried to follow him, but he threw the bolt on the door and took another shot through the maple. The shot missed me by an inch or two.

"Enough," I shouted. "This is enough." I aimed at where the bolt should have been and fired. "I'm tired. I'm sweating. My foot hurts. I'm getting too damn old for this, and I goddamn don't want to kill you."

The bolt gave and I threw my shoulder at the door. It swung open, and the killer stood there next to an overstuffed chair, his gun aimed at a door across the room and not at me. Mine was aimed at him. It didn't seem like a stalemate to me.

"You know who's in that closet?" he said feverishly. His hand was shaking.

"Parkman," I guessed.

"Parkman," he agreed.

"If you don't put your gun down, I'll shoot and keep shooting. The closet's small and I don't think there's much chance even I would miss from here."

"What makes you think I care if you shoot Parkman?" I said, holding my gun on a line with his chest.

"You care, Peters, for God's sake," came Parkman's muffled voice from inside the closet. "Do what he wants."

"I can't do what he wants," I shouted so Parkman could hear me. "If I put down my gun, he shoots you and me."

"I haven't killed him yet," said the shaking killer.

"Let me guess why," I said. "Could be a couple of things. You haven't got the stomach for it. Shooting two killers and Lipparini is one thing, but an innocent man is another. On the other hand, maybe you've been toying with the idea of finding some way to get rid of Parkman and make it look like he killed himself, knowing he'd get caught for killing the two at the gym."

"Thanks," groaned Parkman inside the closet. "Thanks a lot. Give him ideas. I don't have enough problems here without you coming in and giving him ideas."

"Like I said outside, put it down and come down the hill with me. Either that or I'm going to have to shoot you."

"Hey," sobbed Parkman. "What about me?"

"There's no reason to shoot Parkman," I reasoned. "But if that's the way you want to go out, go ahead."

The shaking gun turned suddenly in my direction, or roughly in my direction, and kicked red, white, and loud three times. Inside the closet Parkman screamed. I didn't shoot. The first two bullets he fired hit the ceiling. The last one took a piece of my right ear. A steady gun would have killed me. If he'd had another shot or two, that might have killed me too, but he was dry. I put my gun in my belt and tried to hide the exasperation in my voice as I said, "Is that enough? I can't afford to keep this up till you get lucky. Look at my ear."

He looked at me, dropped his gun, and hurtled himself in my direction with a "Damn you." He fought about as well as he could shoot. I wasn't worried about a broken hand. I was no pro like Joe Louis and I had a lot to be angry about. I caught him with a short right to the cheek as I stepped to the side and another to the kidney as he tried to straighten up. If Ruby Goldstein or some other honest ref had been there, I would have been disqualified.

"Enough?" I said, looking down at him.

He held his possibly broken jaw as he tried to stand, and said, with a tear in his voice, "Enough."

"What's going on out there?" shouted Parkman. "What the hell's—"

"I won," I shouted. "I'll let you out in a minute."

"A minute? A minute? I've been in here for days, goddamn it!"

"Shut up," I shouted, and helped the killer to his wobbly legs and into the stuffed chair.

"Thanks," he said. "You think my jaw is broken?"

"No," I said helpfully. "I don't think you'd be talking if it was, but I could be wrong."

"I should have been more patient last night when you were taking that shower," he said. "I'm not good at this."

"You were bad at it," I admitted, "but you did have a few lucky breaks. You want to tell me about it before we go down?"

Ralph Howard pushed back his white hair with a clean palm and told me his story.

10

"**Y**ou'd better take care of your ear," he said before he began. I thanked him, found a towel in the small bathroom, and clamped it against my head as I sat across from him in a wooden rocking chair and listened.

"I invested heavily in a stable of boxers," he said, reaching up to adjust a tie that was usually there but wasn't any longer. "I didn't know it would be so damn expensive. I kept sinking more and more into it with less to show for my investment. There was always the chance of a big fight, a decent purse, but they never came. Instead of making money I found myself supporting the families of six boxers, none of whom proved to be particularly impressive. The advice of Mr. Parkman was greatly responsible for my situation."

"I heard that," Parkman shouted. "I was straight with you. I was straight with him, Peters. That's the God's—"

"Al," I yelled. "Shut up."

"Then Lipparini approached me at a restaurant," Ralph went on.

I checked to see if the bleeding had stopped. The towel was soaked. My ear was still bleeding.

"Lipparini," said Ralph, "was very sympathetic. He'd heard about my fighters, my situation, and said he wanted to help, that he could help with money but that he couldn't get directly involved in ownership of fighters. It sounded good."

"So you agreed," I prompted.

"Obviously," he said. "If I hadn't, we wouldn't be here

now. Lipparini put up money and remained in the background for all of two weeks, at which time he made clear what his plan was. I was to use my social and business connections to arrange for fights between professional boxers in the Army and my fighters. Exhibitions would be fine."

"And you couldn't do it?"

"I tried to explain to him that I could not use the connections I had made through Trans World. Using our government contacts to make such connections would almost certainly fail and might result in my losing my job and reputation."

"And Lipparini wouldn't listen," I said.

"He wouldn't listen. He gave me deadlines, told me I had to pay back the money he had put up, even sent someone to try to frighten me. Almost ran me down on the street. Anne was with me."

"I know," I said. "And you . . ."

". . . decided there was nothing to do but die," he said. "I'd made contact with those two . . ."

"Silvio and Mush," I supplied. "The ones you shot at Reed's."

"They seemed willing enough to listen to my plan," Ralph said, running his hand against his jaw. "And I thought it would be safe. They wouldn't help me and then tell Lipparini. They were as frightened of him as I was."

"So," I cut in, checking my ear again, which seemed to have stopped bleeding, "you put up the last of your cash to pay them to beat some poor bum to death who happened to look like you. They gave him your clothes, shaved and showered him, and then smashed his face in and dumped him on the beach. The only problem was that they ran into Joe Louis doing some late roadwork on the shore, and he saw them."

"And you came along," Ralph added.

"And I came along," I agreed. "Ralph, putting aside the fact that you paid to have some innocent jerk killed, didn't you think about fingerprints, teeth?"

"No," he admitted. "I didn't think anyone would doubt it was me if the body was found on my beach, in my clothes. And I'd let Anne know that I was worried."

"You were right," I said, throwing the towel in the corner. "No one even thought about it, but Mush and Silvio told you that Louis had seen them. And they probably called you the morning after Lipparini talked to me and let you know that the pressure was on them. Did they want more money?"

"Yes." Ralph nodded. "I didn't have any more to give them. Not enough to make a difference. I told them I'd give them five thousand each if they killed you. Then I followed you and made my way to Parkman's office."

"You waited long enough for them to kill me," I reminded him.

"At that point," he said, "I wouldn't have minded. I'm being truthful."

"That doesn't make you a nice person," I reminded him. "When I went out in the gym with Louis, you stepped in, shot the two of them on the floor, and went out the window with Parkman."

"Speaking of whom," Parkman moaned from the closet, "I would appreciate getting—"

"Why did you try to kill me?" I asked. "I wasn't getting close to you."

"But you were getting close to Anne," he said, looking directly at me. "It was you she sent for when she thought she needed help. It was you who spent the night with her two days after I was dead."

"You aren't dead," I reminded him.

"But she thought I was. And then she gave you my clothes. I threw my life away so she could have the insurance, and she lets you through the door before my . . . the body is fully cold."

"And that's why you tried to kill me at the Ocean Breeze, why you tore up my clothes?"

"My clothes," Ralph countered. "Not your clothes. My wife, not your wife. Your ex-wife."

"And you want me to give a little grudging admiration at this point," I said. "All your sacrifices, for wife and empire, that kind of crap? You killed some poor bum and ran to keep Lipparini from getting your skin or the police from throwing the key away and your friends from knowing what you were mixed up in. You dumped Anne and went off to start clean, but it was too dirty."

"I left her with more than you did when you were divorced," he said. "This is getting us nowhere. Let Parkman out and we'll go. I really have nothing more to say to you."

"Not that easy," I said, getting out of the rocker and moving to the closet. "You show up now and Anne loses the money, you, and her self-respect. She has to live with all the crap you've spread around."

I turned the key and opened the closet door. Parkman blinked in the sudden light like a rat with a flashlight in his face. His face was dirty, his flashy green suit jacket on the floor, and his shirt open. He twitched and stepped forward. "What the hell," he grumbled, and when he spotted Ralph, "I'm going to sue you, you bastard."

Ralph looked up at the angry man and laughed, not a mean laugh but the laugh of a man giving in to hysteria.

"Sit down, Al," I said. "I've got a plan to make us all happy. I'll get Howard's wife to pay you the money he owes you. She'll want to make good on his IOUs."

Ralph had stopped laughing suddenly and looked up. There were tears of laughter on his cheeks.

"And what do I do in exchange for this?" Parkman said. "I'm not letting him go. I let him go and the cops think I hit Silvio and Mush, the cops and Lipparini's bunch. No, you go turn him in and I walk out of this losing a grand instead of my life."

"All I'm asking for, Al," I said, "is to give Ralph the opportunity to turn himself in."

"Why?" Parkman asked, wandering around the room. "He killed people all over the place. He was going to kill you and me."

"His wife's a decent woman," I said. "You keep your mouth shut and stay out of the way till tomorrow and you get two thousand dollars and my appreciation."

"Cash," Parkman said. "No check. Cash. Saturday at the latest."

"No," I said. "You might have to wait a while for her to put that kind of money together. No more insurance coming in, remember. She might get a few bucks for this cabin, but not four thousand."

"I've got your marker on this, Peters?" Parkman said.

"You've got it," I agreed. "Go down the hill. You'll find my car at the bottom in some trees off to the left. I'll be right there."

Parkman tried to regain some dignity by retrieving his jacket from the closet and sneering at Ralph, but Ralph wasn't paying any attention. I waited till we heard Parkman going down the hill before I turned to Ralph.

"I'll meet you on the beach near your house at sundown," I said. "I'll keep things quiet, not a word to anyone. You meet me, and we go up to the house and you turn yourself in. I'll prepare Anne for it before you get there."

"And if I say no?" he asked.

I didn't bother to answer. I left him sitting there and followed Parkman down the hill. Ralph could have a few hours to think about it, and I'd have time to make a few calls.

I gave Parkman fifty bucks and dropped him at a hotel in Long Beach, telling him to stay in the room till someone came for him. He complained, but I reminded him of the two thousand and he shut up.

Then I went up Pacific Coast to Sepulveda and found a diner in El Segundo. I made my phone calls and ordered a couple of cheeseburgers, fries, and a strawberry shake. When they came I was surprised that my appetite was gone. I got one burger and the shake down. I shoved the second burger and the fries at a kid who was eating a hot dog. He took them with a grown up "Thanks" followed by, "What happened to you, mister?"

"A raccoon bit me," I said, and went for the door.

I made it to Santa Monica with about an hour to spare. Anne opened the door.

"Explain," she said. She was wearing a black skirt and sweater and a determined look.

"I think we'll have Ralph's killer soon," I said. "Maybe tonight."

"I told you," she said, stepping back so I could come in, "that won't bring Ralph back."

I considered saying, "You never can tell," but kept my mouth shut.

"The funeral's tomorrow," she said. "Will you be going?"

"I'll go to Ralph's funeral," I said.

She stood in the hallway, her hands folded across her breasts, the dwindling light from the sun shining on her and giving her a red tinge. She looked beautiful.

"Now," she went on, "why all the questions about Ralph's cabin and places we—"

"A mistake," I said, stepping past her toward the kitchen. "One of my dumb mistakes. Can I have something to eat?"

"Anjelica's gone for the day," she said, shaking her head. "I'll make you a sandwich."

Through the window I could see the sun going down. She made a tuna sandwich, and I ate. Then I drank a beer and a coffee till the sun was just about gone. If someone knocked at the door, I'd have to do some fast explaining, some very fast explaining, but I wasn't going to do that until I was sure.

"I can't—" she started to say, and then was stopped by a quartet of sounds outside. They might have been a backfiring truck, but they weren't.

"What?" she said.

"Probably nothing," I said casually, trying to keep the sandwich and the beer down. "I'll go take a look. You have some cake or something? I'm really hungry."

"I'll look around," she said wearily, and I walked slowly toward the front door. It was hard to walk slowly, but I did. When I got to the porch I ran. I could see someone on the beach, but the sun was gone and I couldn't see clearly who it was until I was about twenty feet away.

There was a man standing there with a gun in his hand. Another man was lying in the sand, no more than five or six feet from where I'd found the body three nights earlier. This time the body really was Ralph Howard's.

"Son a bitch came up the beach and shot at me," Jerry Genette said, turning his gun at me. "You set me up."

"Hold it," I said. "I didn't set you up. He was supposed to meet me on the beach and turn himself in. I told you. He thought you were me."

"And he tried to kill you?" he asked. "You set me up."

The gun came up at my chest.

"Ralph Howard couldn't hit a Jap sub if it came up the beach and stopped two feet in front of him. I told you Lipparini's killer would be here and you could bring him in, make yourself a hero to the good guys and bad guys."

"You knew he'd try to kill you," Genette said between clenched teeth.

"I figured he might," I admitted. "I hoped he wouldn't."

I said it, but I wasn't sure I meant it. Ralph Howard lying there dead wasn't much easier to explain than Ralph Howard knocking at the door and saying, "I'm home dear, what's for dessert?"

"I'm not going to forget this, Peters," Genette said.

"What are you so upset about?" I asked reasonably. "When the cops come, I'll explain it was all self-defense. They'll understand."

"I'm not staying here to talk to cops," Genette said. "I've got a better idea."

"I've got some friends up at the house watching," I said, looking back as the lights went on in the house. "Let's make a deal. You take Howard's body away and make it disappear, and we forget about the whole thing. You have Lipparini's killer, and I have a case of amnesia."

He looked up and down the beach for a few seconds, chewed on the inside of his lip, thought about it, and said, "Okay."

I walked up to the house without looking back and went in. My knees were trembling and my foot was throbbing when I got to the kitchen and saw the slice of chocolate cake.

"What was it?" Anne said, pouring coffee.

"Nothing, truck," I said, holding my hands under the table to keep them from shaking.

"Well," she said with a smile, "you're in luck. I found your favorite, chocolate cake."

"My favorite," I agreed, and wondered how I was going to get past the next few minutes.

I left an hour later and called Parkman at the hotel in Long Beach.

"Al, Howard is dead. Lipparini's people got to him. You're off the hook. They know he killed Mush, Silvio, and Lipparini and not you. A cop named Meara is going to come and get you later tonight. You tell him you got scared when Mush and Silvio got shot and you ran. You've been holed up since then."

"Wait," he said.

"Howard is really dead now," I explained. "The widow will collect the insurance."

"You got a deal," he said. "Do me a favor. Don't let me see you again."

He hung up, and I drove to the Santa Monica police station, asked the desk man, who was reading a *Collier's*, where Meara's office was, and found my way. He was down a hallway on the main floor, a dark hallway. The door was dark wood. I knocked and Meara bellowed, "No one locks the damn doors in a police station, Peters."

I walked in. Meara was sitting behind the desk with his feet up on it. His jacket was off and his shoulder holster rested on his stomach. He was drinking from a coffee cup, but from the look on his face I didn't think there was coffee in the cup.

"I'll tell you where Parkman is," I said.

He laughed, took a drink, and shook his head. "Parkman," he said. "Parkman. I just got a report on our friend on the beach. You remember our friend on the beach, the one you and your nigger found."

He took another drink.

"I remember," I said. "Howard . . ."

"No," he said holding his belly. "Not Howard. Unless Howard had all his teeth pulled out and bought cheap dentures about five or six years back. If he did, Howard's dentist is going to want to know whose teeth he was working on for the last decade or two."

"So—" I started.

"Where is Howard and who is the guy with the dentures?" He took another big drink and finished what was in the cup. "You want a drink? Eighty proof Chase and Sanborn . . ."

"No thanks," I said. "Howard's dead. Lipparini's people caught up with him. Howard killed Lipparini and those two guys at Reed's."

"No go, Peters," he said, yanking a bottle out of his drawer and sitting up to pour it. "You could be pulling something with Howard and the grieving widow. There's insurance money going down here."

"And you want some of it."

He threw the bottle at me and stood up. "You start that kind of shit and I'll bite off the other ear. You prove

Howard's dead, and I don't care if she collects. All I want to be sure of is nobody gets away with killing people."

"A body will turn up tomorrow," I said. "No face, like the guy on the beach, but this one will have a mouthful of teeth."

"If it doesn't happen," he said, swaying behind the desk, "I come looking for you. You know, Peters, I like it better when it ends this way. No fast lawyers getting people short terms, no long trials. Cleaner this way, but the body better turn up."

"It will," I said.

"I'll hold on to Parkman for a day or two just in case," he said with a grin on his pink face. "If there's no body, Parkman and I go to the library and he tells what he knows and no insurance and some bad nights for the widow. You wouldn't want bad nights for the widow?"

I gave him my own nasty grin and told him where to find Parkman. I had just turned my back when Meara spoke behind me. "I tell you I got a kid in the Army, Peters?"

"Yeah, Meara, you told me."

"He's the only kid we got. Could get himself killed."

I went through the door and got out of Santa Monica. The airport wasn't far and I could just make it.

11

Joe Louis was in a little room inside the airport not far from where Trans World Flight 29 would soon be taking off for Chicago with connections to New York. When I went in, he was in his uniform, shoes polished, looking out of a small window at the planes taking off. According to the woman who had led me to the room, the Champ was in there instead of in the regular waiting room to protect him from fans who might recognize him.

"It's all over, Champ," I said as he turned to face me.

He listened quietly while I told him the tale, leaving out some of the details. I had the feeling that he didn't care much, that there were other things on his mind. All he was really interested in was that he was off the hook.

"You could use a good cut man," he said, looking at my face and ragged ear. "You're a mess, worse than I looked after the first Schmeling fight."

"You bounced back," I said. "I can do it. I just heal a little slower as I age. It goes with the body."

"I guess," he said. "How much I owe you?" He had his hand under his Army jacket and on his wallet when I stopped him.

"You don't owe me anything," I said. "I owe you a refund. You overpaid, Champ."

He took his hand off his wallet and gave me a puzzled look. "First time anybody ever said no when I had my hand on my wallet," he said. "You ain't a rich man."

"I ain't a rich man," I agreed. "But I like to think I'm not a thief either. Next time you're in L.A. after the war and you've got a fight, leave two tickets for me at the box office, if you remember."

"I'll remember," he said, and then he paused as if he had something more to come out with and didn't know how to say it. "You got any kids?" he asked.

"No kids, no wife," I said.

"I talked to Marva, that's my wife, this morning after the police finished talking to me. We're going to have a baby. I'm gonna be a father."

"Great," I said, holding out a hand.

He took it with a small smile. "I like kids," he said. "I'm gonna try to put things together, be a good husband, father, you know?"

He was playing with the Army cap in his hands, rolling it into a cylinder and unrolling it in his big hands.

"It's hard," he said, shaking his head. "I can train, do the running, eat the food, get the sleep. Always do what Chappie told me, but he's gone. Then when the women come or some friend needs a few hundred dollars, I can't say no, haven't got the will for that. I gotta work on it."

Never having had the problem of women eagerly pursuing me or friends after my wealth, I strained my imagination and came up blank.

"You'll manage," I said lamely.

"I'll try," he said. "Sure you don't want . . ."

"I'm sure," I said.

There was a knock at the door, and the woman who had led me to the room stuck her head in and said it was time for the flight to Chicago.

"Could have taken a military flight," Louis said, "but I want to get back by morning. I've got that exhibition tomorrow."

I nodded. He looked as if he had something more to say but didn't know the words. He picked up his green duffle bag at the door, put it over his shoulder, said, "Thanks," and went out the door.

Half an hour later I was in bed dreaming dreams I didn't remember or want to remember.

A knock at the door woke me in the morning. The knock was followed by the appearance of Mrs. Plaut. I sat up.

"Phone," she said succinctly.

"Thanks," I said, trying to rise.

"You look worse than Elliott Sylvester," she said, examining my face as I groped for my pants.

"I don't want to know who Elliott Sylvester is," I said.

"Elliott Sylvester," she said, "was our neighbor when we lived in the Valley. He engaged in combat with a cougar."

My pants were on backwards. I turned them around and ran my tongue over my lower lip, but it still felt dry.

"It was his idea," Mrs. Plaut explained. "He was of the opinion that he could best a cougar in combat as he had bested many of the neighbor boys in wrestling, but that was foolhardy."

"At best," I agreed, standing up and feeling my wounds tremble with delight at the torment they had planned for me this sunny day.

"Cougars are much more dangerous than young men," she said.

"I'll bear that in mind," I said as I stumbled toward the door. She gave way and let me pass but followed me down the landing to the pay phone. I picked up the dangling receiver and said something I hoped sounded like "Hello."

"Peters?" Meara said. "You sound like shit."

"Thanks."

"Body turned up this morning," he said. "Guy around fifty-five or so, flannel shirt. Shot and thrown off the rocks up near Santa Barbara. Not much to identify."

"That's too bad," I said.

"Too bad," he agreed. "Parkman's on his way home. Keep your ass out of Santa Monica."

"Does that mean we're not playing quoits tonight?" I tried.

He didn't bother to answer. The phone went dead.

I turned to Mrs. Plaut, who was watching me.

"Somebody died," I explained.

"It is inevitable," she said. "Happens to everyone, especially relatives. The man with the hair is waiting for you downstairs."

"Thanks," I said, but she didn't hear me. She had already turned and started down the stairs. I went to the railing and looked down at Seidman.

We didn't talk much on the way to the Wilshire Station. I asked him how his dental work was going and he said it looked as if he wouldn't have to kill Shelly.

Phil was just saying good-bye to a chunky woman with an angry look on her face who could have been anything from forty to sixty. She was clutching her black patent leather purse to her chest with two hands to keep any snatcher in the police station from getting it.

"I'll have a man on it this afternoon, Mrs. Courtney," he said with a smile that made him look as if he had been interrupted by painful stomach gas.

"It should have been attended to weeks ago," she said. "If it had been, I wouldn't have had to complain to my congressman."

"This afternoon," Phil said, tugging at his collar.

"We will see," said Mrs. Courtney, who turned and hurried down the hall, after giving me a look that told me I was just what she expected in a place like this.

"Neighbor's using her garden hose without permission," Phil said, his teeth clenched. "That's the kind of shit I have to . . . Come in."

Seidman and I went in.

"You want coffee?" Phil growled. "Or iodine. You can drink the iodine and rub the coffee on your face, or what's left of it."

"Just the coffee," I said.

Seidman volunteered to get it and went out of the room.

"Explain," Phil said. "Explain fast before Steve gets back. The less crap he has to hear, the less he has to lie about it."

I talked fast and told the truth, down to Howard's killing and the body Meara had told me about less than an hour before.

"You know what I should do?" he said, holding up a clenched right fist. "I should make you completely unrecognizable. You've got me, the department, yourself, up to the balls in fraud."

"I wanted Anne to have the insurance money," I said. "The money and some decent memories of her second husband. Who did it hurt?"

"It didn't do Howard a hell of a lot of good," Phil said. "And you don't look too hot either, not that I give a damn."

Seidman came back through the door with the coffee, a cup for each of us. Phil took a gulp, swished it around his mouth, and let it go down. Then he put the cup on his desk and ran a thick paw over his clipped hair before he looked at the stack of reports and files on his desk.

"Here's how it goes down," he said. "The two guys in the gym and Lipparini, killers unknown. Looks like an intersquad gang mess." He looked up for an argument and got none from Seidman or me.

"Howard was killed on the beach Sunday by the guys who got it at Reed's. Maybe the mob didn't like their killing Howard, or they were covering up. Maybe . . . The whole goddamn thing is full of holes."

I could tell from the still clenched fist that he wanted to hit something or someone, possibly the departed Mrs. Courtney. Instead, he picked up his coffee cup and took another gulp.

"It'll hold," Seidman said. "And we get to put all that back in the records room."

Phil looked at the reports and nodded agreement. "Sure," he said. "We've got more important things to do, like stakeouts on Westwood retirees who borrow garden hoses. Get out, Toby."

"I'm sorry, Phil," I said, putting down my unfinished coffee.

It was the wrong thing to say. He didn't want my sympathy. Our brotherhood was not based on mutual support but on a thin thread of antagonism. His face went beet red and he stepped around the desk. Seidman stepped in front of him, and I got the hell out of Phil's office.

When I got to the Farraday Building, Jeremy was in the lobby putting new name tags on the directory board. For a few years he'd had the names printed at a place across the street. Recently, Alice Pallice had churned out the little tabs on her machine. The turnover in the Farraday was so fast that it was a major chore.

"Admiral Farragut left," Jeremy said, stepping back to see if the tab he had just inserted was aligned with the one above.

Admiral Farragut was the nickname I had given a tenant who moved in less than a month earlier. He always dressed in white and looked a little like the pictures of Sir Thomas Lipton on the tea boxes, right down to the little white goatee beard. From his small office on the second floor, Admiral Farragut had given illegal goat gland injections to aged ladies and gentlemen who wanted one more shot at being young. Apparently, there weren't enough seekers of the Fountain of Youth in the neighborhood to make it worth while, so he had packed up his elixir and headed north, south, or east. He couldn't go any further west.

"Would you like his office?" Jeremy said, putting in another name tab.

I could afford it, at least till what was left of Joe Louis's money ran out. The temptation was great.

"I would charge you no more than you are paying for your share of Minck's suite," he continued, delicately adjusting a small tab with his huge fingers.

"Thanks, Jeremy," I said. "I'll think about it. You going to do that exhibition?"

"I'll wrestle the soldiers," he said, reaching into his pocket for yet another name tab, "but no poetry. If I cannot subject my own work to ridicule, I cannot do it to Byron or Emily Dickinson. I've struck an alternative deal. Alice and I will distribute copies of *Wings of the White Dove* to all servicemen following the exhibition."

"Sounds like a good deal," I said, moving toward the stairs. "I'll get back to you about the office."

Shelly was listening to Fred Waring and the Pennsylvanians on the radio and working on a patient when I came in. He turned and looked at me, leaving the woman in the chair with her mouth open.

"My suit," he said.

I fished forty dollars out of my pocket and handed it to him. "You can buy three suits for that if you shop carefully," I said.

"I'm not angry anymore," he said magnanimously, tucking the money into the pocket of his stained white jacket.

"I'm relieved," I said, heading for my office. "Better take care of the lady."

Shelly turned to look at the woman as if he had forgotten she was there. She looked frightened, and he turned back to me. "Mildred is coming back this morning," he said.

"Fortune smiles on you, Sheldon," I said.

He scratched his neck and looked at his fingernails to see if they told him anything, possibly something about cleaning them. He decided they didn't.

"Mildred and I need a vacation together," he said. "Don't you think?"

I shrugged and he looked at the woman in the chair, who shook her head to indicate she thought Shelly and Mildred needed a vacation together, or anything else the man holding the sharp instruments might need or want.

"You mind if I use this money on a weekend with Mildred?" he asked. "I've got two other suits."

"Be my guest," I said. "Might be a good idea before it's too late. I hear they're drafting overage dentists. You might be working on some colonel's teeth in Manila by June."

Shelly's glasses dropped dangerously on his nose. "I'm too old," he said, looking from me to the woman, who, mouth open, heartily agreed that he was too old. "I'm overweight, near-sighted, and out of touch with the latest techniques."

"And those are his good points," I told the woman in the chair.

"I'd look terrible in a uniform," he went on.

"You looked fine as a waiter," I said. "They'd make you an officer. Lieutenant Sheldon Minck."

"No," bleated Shelly.

The panic in his face was more than I had expected, and I didn't want to be responsible for what his trembling hands might do to the woman in the chair.

"Relax, Sheldon," I said. "I'm joking. You're safe, free to continue your humanitarian work right here."

"That's a joke?" he shouted. "That's his idea of a joke," he said to the woman in the chair, who made a face to make it clear that she thought my joke was in terrible taste. It was at that point that I decided to turn down Jeremy's offer of a new office. I'd miss Shelly too much. He was family.

"Can you imagine that?" he said, turning to the woman in the chair. "If I told you all that I've done for him, you'd call me a saint."

I went into my office and sat down. Shelly had left no messages on the desk, but the mail was sitting there. I went through it and discovered that I owed a refund to a woman in Bakersfield who claimed I had failed to find her lost cat. She wanted her twenty dollars back. I considered writing to her to tell her that I hadn't promised to find her cat, only to look for it. There were no promises in my business, at least none you could be sure of keeping. The hell with it. J. Pierpont Peters stuffed a twenty into an envelope, addressed it to Miss Merle Levine in Bakersfield, and ended the correspondence.

Later in the morning I would call Anne and try to talk her into paying Parkman two grand when the insurance money on Ralph came in. I didn't want to, but I also knew I'd go to the funeral for Ralph and watch them lower some other guy into the ground. I didn't know where they planned to plant the real Ralph Howard.

Hell, the mail was more interesting. A company in Porterville wanted to know if I would be interested in a career as a plumber. With all the plumbers in the armed services, the world was looking for people who could control the flow of water. Women were encouraged to consider the possibilities of a new career in a challenging field that had previously been for men only.

I wondered what was going to happen when the war ended and all those men, at least those who could still walk and talk and handle tools, wanted their jobs back: plumbing, mechanicing, selling, preaching, and teaching. It even struck me that some of them might be shell-shocked enough to consider being private detectives. Unless we had a post-war boom of private crime, there wouldn't be enough cheating, violence, and runaway wives to go around. Then again, I might not have to worry about it. By the time the war ended, I might have enough to retire. At the rate I was going, if the war stopped in four or five years I'd have a nice little nest egg of a couple hundred dollars.

I was starting to feel sorry for myself, which was a bad sign for a battered detective. I decided to go out and needle Shelly a little more. I checked the money in the drawer, noticed that it had started to rain, and went into the outer office, where Shelly was irritatedly telling the woman, "Spit, don't swallow. You're choking cause you're not listening. You spit that stuff out. Who wants to swallow it? Some people have no—"

And then Shelly spotted me. He reached for his unlit cigar while the woman behind him gagged.

"You had a message," Shelly said, plunging his hand in his pocket. "Got it right here. Almost forgot when you came in and started to taunt me. See what happens when you do that?"

The woman behind him sounded like she was trying to down a whole orange.

"Spit, spit," Shelly said to her over his shoulder as he chomped on his cigar and looked in his pockets for the message. He found it and grinned as he handed it to me.

I flattened the crumpled sheet and tried to read Shelly's scrawl.

"Marion Morrison called me?" I said.

"Yeah," he said. "If my name were Marion and I was a guy, which I am, I'd change it to Jim or—"

"Shelly," I suggested. Then I asked, "And I'm supposed to get to the Alhambra Arms right away?"

"That's what he said," Shelly agreed. "You ask me, I wouldn't meet guys named Marion in hotels."

"I'll keep that in mind," I said, heading for the door. I didn't bother to stop and tell Shelly that Marion Morrison was the real name of an actor named John Wayne.